THE DEADLY FEAST

JUMPSTART DUCHY
BOOK 4

STEFON MEARS

Thousand Faces Publishing

Also by Stefon Mears

The Rise of Magic Series
Magician's Choice
Sleight of Mind
Lunar Alchemy
Three Fae Monte
The Sphinx Principle
Double Backed Magic
Mercury Fold (coming soon)

Cavan Oltblood Series
Half a Wizard
The Ice Dagger
Spells of Undeath

Power City Tales
Not Quite Bulletproof
No Money in Heroism

Standalones
Between the Cracks
Sects and the City
Prince of a Thousand Worlds
Devil's Night
Portal-Land, Oregon
Stealing from Pirates
Fade to Gold
With a Broken Sword
Twice Against the Dragon
The House on Cedar Street
Sudden Death
On the Edge of Faerie

Short Story Collections
Spell Slingers
Twisted Timelines
Longhairs and Short Tales: A Collection of Cat Stories
Confronting Legends (Spells & Swords Vol. 1)
The Patreon Collection, Vol. 1-8 (Vol. 9, coming soon)

Nonfiction
The 30-Day Novel and Beyond!

Spells for Hire Series
Devil's Shoestring
Zombie Powder
Spirit Trap
Dragon's Blood

The Telepath Trilogy
Surviving Telepathy
Immoral Telepathy
Targeting Telepathy

Edge of Humanity Series
Caught Between Monsters
Hunting Monsters

Jumpstart Duchy Series
Into the Torn Kingdoms
The Dragon's Gold
The Gift Castle
The Deadly Feast
The King's Test
Triumph in the Torn Kingdoms

Published by Thousand Faces Publishing, Portland, Oregon

http://1kfaces.com

Copyright © 2022 by Stefon Mears

Front cover image © Pavle Matic | Dreamstime.com (File ID: 123414986)

All rights reserved.

The characters and events in this book are fictitious. Any resemblance to real persons, living or dead, is coincidental and not intended by the author.

No part of this book may be reproduced in any form or by any electronic or mechanical means, including information storage and retrieval systems, without written permission from the author, except for the use of brief quotations in a book review.

Hardback ISBN: 978-1-948490-46-7

Paperback ISBN: 978-1-948490-33-7

THE DEADLY FEAST

FOREWORD

The man known as Aefric Brightstaff was not born on Qorunn. He was born on the distant world of Earth, where he went by the name Keifer McShane.

On Earth, he knew the world of Qorunn only through *The Torn Kingdoms*, the setting of his favorite roleplaying game. His primary source of joy and solace, following the untimely death of his wife, Andi.

When a Jumpstart crowdfunding campaign for the next edition of *The Torn Kingdoms* offered him the chance to become a duke in the world he loved, Keifer pounced on it. Imagined they would send him a patent of nobility. Ask his opinion about the non-player character who'd bear his name and title. Perhaps even allow him to include Andi as his duchess, when the books went to print.

He couldn't wait to become a part of the world he loved so well.

But he mistook it all for make-believe.

Keifer didn't expect the great Mage of Marrisford himself, the one and only Kainemorton, to show up on his doorstep.

Keifer didn't expect to be transported to Qorunn, where he would start life anew as an orphan boy on the streets of the fabled city of Sartis. That shining beacon on the southern sea.

Now known as Aefric, he grew into a powerful adventurer. Widely believed to be a wizard, he is in fact the first of the dweomerblood. It is said that magic itself flows through his very veins.

As Aefric, he mastered the fabled Brightstaff. He fought in the Godswalk Wars, and saved countless lives at the Battle of Deepwater, in the kingdom of Armyr.

In gratitude, King Colm of Armyr named Aefric Duke of Deepwater. And no sooner had Aefric taken possession of his duchy than he prevented an invasion by Armyr's southern neighbor, Malimfar.

Since then, he has worked to unite his vassals. To heal his lands and his peoples from the damage done by the Godswalk Wars. To fight off assassins, slavers and smugglers. To deal with foreign intrigues and the influence of the pirate queen, Nelazzi.

All while being pressured to marry, and sire an heir who will one day inherit his duchy...

Keifer McShane. Aefric Brightstaff.

One man who has lived two lives.

This is book four of his story...

1

Aefric Brightstaff awoke suddenly in a bed that was not his own. Old instincts fed adrenaline through his system, waking him completely as his eyes darted about. Unsure for the moment where he was. And why.

He lay on a mattress well-stuffed with soft feathers. Sheets that weren't silk, but close enough to tell him he wasn't in a cell, or some roadside inn.

The windows were shuttered closed, but that likely didn't matter much. The cracks around them were dark. Not yet dawn. Depending on the moon, the shutters could have stood wide open and not offered much more light.

He could brighten the room with a spell, of course, but light might draw unwanted attention. Besides. His eyes had adjusted well enough to the dark. He could see the chamber about him in shades of gray.

The walls, floor and ceiling were stone — mostly gray, even when lit, he now recalled. Woven carpets on the floor.

Carpets of ... reds and blues. Was that right? He thought it was. And from the sweet scent, fresh herbs had been scattered underneath those carpets recently.

An armoire. Oak. Copper wash basin, with a pair of ewers for water, as well as towels, soaps, and a razor.

Luggage in front of the armoire. Two trunks. Both … his? Yes. His.

The next sight made him sigh with relief.

The Brightstaff stood tall beside the bed. Next to an oak night table, but not leaning against it. Comfortably close at hand.

The Brightstaff, Aefric's namesake, was more than six feet of white thunderwood — about his own height — with a worn, brown leather wrap where he most often held the staff. Embedded in its top, a yellow diamond about the size of his thumb.

Reassured by the presence of his favorite tool and weapon — as well as his apparently undisturbed luggage — he continued looking about.

A good-sized hearth, with no fire blazing because it was still summer. Late summer now, but still summer. The room was neither too hot nor too cold. Something to do with the background buzz of magic all about him.

A buzz that he recognized.

It was the magic of clay and stone, balancing the temperature of the room. Pulling heat from within the surface of Qorunn when needed, and shunting excess heat down and away when appropriate.

Fine, skillful work by a dedicated *vohlcairn*, a wizard who focused almost entirely on the magic of clay and stone.

Of course. Late summer. A castle room whose temperature was controlled by a *vohlcairn*.

He was in Norrtarr, in the barony of Norra. Safe within the castle of one of his own vassals. Because he was no longer Aefric Brightstaff, wandering adventurer.

Ever since this past spring, he was now his grace, Ser Aefric Brightstaff, Duke of Deepwater and Baron of Netar. Not to mention a couple of other honorifics that were often included alongside his name.

Part of the reason he carried so much luggage these days. He had appearances to maintain. So he rarely went anywhere without several changes of clothes, as well as other things he might need.

He carried more than usual for this trip, because he'd come to Norra for the Feast of Dereth Sehk. And he wasn't entirely sure what would be expected of him, over the days that followed.

He eased back down on the mattress. Thinking about the politics and pageantry to come over the next few days. He was awake now, and he might as well—

A small, feminine sound of protest came from beside him in bed, and a woman rolled over and snuggled in against his chest. She nuzzled his shoulder like a scent-marking cat, trailing long, loose curls in her wake. Chestnut curls, though he knew that more by memory than by sight in the dim light.

She settled down with a happy sigh.

Octave. Pretty Octave, with her lavender scent, her wide blue eyes and her soft, tanned skin. A young serving woman here at Norrtarr, in his bed tonight providing him *leaba*. The pleasures of a bedmate, freely offered by a commoner to a visiting, titled Armyrian noble.

It had been Octave who'd first introduced the old tradition to Aefric, this past spring, when he'd come through on the way to his new ducal seat at Water's End.

She'd come to his rooms that night. Explained the tradition patiently. Answered all his questions. Waited with bated breath to hear whether Aefric would accept her offer or send her away.

He'd accepted. An eye-opening experience in many ways.

And now, tonight, Aefric had once more returned to Norrtarr for a single night. He hadn't been sure what to expect. He'd considered the possibility, of course, that he'd spend that night alone. As he had so often, when he was an adventurer.

But nights alone were not common among the nobility of Armyr. When traveling, a titled noble might be offered *leaba*, but whether at home or on the road, any member of the nobility — no matter how great or small, no matter single or married — might go to another noble hoping to share "the noble privilege."

By which Armyrians meant a night of pursuing the bliss moment together for no other reason than pleasure.

It was purely optional. Either party could refuse without insult or loss of face. No gifts were expected or allowed.

As the concept had been explained to Aefric, the nobles had decided some time back that the political risks posed by jealousy and illicit affairs outweighed the need to keep a desirable lover to oneself.

Of course, the development of the bitter nysta tea, which prevented conception when drunk by either or both parties before spending a night together, seemed a likely contributor to the practice.

Either way, where the nobility led, the common folk followed. And in most cities and large towns, the commoners were as likely to go bed hopping as the nobles, these days.

Noble or common, it seemed that Armyrians loved sex.

And none more so than the knights. As far as he could tell, Aefric's Knights of the Lake — the elite of his personal guard — were *all* sleeping together in various configurations.

Another small sound came from Octave, followed by whispered words.

"Your grace is awake. I thought I'd properly exhausted you earlier."

"Sorry," Aefric said, kissing her forehead and stroking the smooth, sleep-warmed skin of her side and flank. "Go back to sleep."

Octave raised up on one elbow. Regarded him with wide eyes that he knew were a pretty shade of blue, though in the dim light they looked pale gray.

She trailed her fingers over Aefric's collarbone. And for a change, not near one of his scars.

"When last I had the pleasure of sharing your grace's bed," she said softly, "you wore a crystal on a thin gold chain. A gift from a lost love. No longer?"

That crystal and its chain were among the few objects he'd brought from Earth, the world in which he'd been born Keifer McShane. Where he'd met a woman named Andrea — Andi, as he usually called her. Where they'd fallen in love, and married.

Where they'd been happy.

Until a car accident took her from him. Sent him into a spiral where the only meager pleasures he retained were in basketball and roleplaying games.

The path that had led him to back Del Baker's Jumpstart campaign for the sixth edition of *The Torn Kingdoms*. Where he'd supported at the "Duke of Deepwater" level, which apparently hadn't been offered to everyone…

"The crystal and chain sit in my rooms at Water's End," Aefric said, voice hushed more by the hour than the topic. "A place of honor. But no longer a constant reminder."

Octave said nothing. Just continued to play her fingers back and forth along his collarbone.

Nevertheless, he felt her question in the air. And decided to answer it.

"As duke, I'm expected to marry and have children. Wouldn't be right for my future bride to see around my neck a constant reminder of a past love."

Octave nodded, still tracing with her fingers.

"When last I shared your grace's bed," she said softly, "the pain of that loss was yet strong. Is it still?"

Aefric reached up and stroked her cheek. "My true healing began that night."

Octave smiled warmly.

"And she who gave me that crystal," he said, "would be grateful to you."

"I was truly the first, after her death?"

That was true and not true. The part of him that had grown up in Qorunn as Aefric had known and loved — briefly — many women. But the part of him that was Keifer hadn't seriously *considered* touching another woman after Andi died.

The true part felt stronger, though.

Aefric nodded. "And a good deal of time had passed."

Octave's eyes moistened. She clutched Aefric for a moment, her face against his chest, while he held her, uncertain what was bothering her.

She looked up, and the tears trailing down her cheeks puzzled him further.

"That your grace went so long ... untouched." She shook her head. "Did no other women even try?"

With Aefric, yes. Certainly. With Keifer, though...

"In truth?" He shrugged. "If they did, I didn't notice."

"Oh, your grace—"

"Keep in mind," Aefric said. "For most of this time, I wasn't a duke. I was just an itinerant adventurer. And I wasn't in Armyr, where seeking the bliss moment is a common pastime."

"Your grace," Octave said firmly. "I could be a tavern wench in Sartis, but if I saw you come in one night, I'd do my best to make sure you left with me."

Aefric chuckled.

"Your grace thinks I jest," she said, half-smiling herself now, as she wiped away her tears. "I do not. In fact, I suspect that many others tried, and your grace didn't notice because they didn't have a good tradition like *leaba* to make their intentions clear."

"Perhaps," Aefric said.

"Speaking of *leaba*, your grace," she said with a different kind of smile altogether. "As you are awake, and so is your bedmate, all that remains is more pleasure."

She trailed her hand down his chest then to stroke someplace lower, and Aefric pulled her into a kiss.

And then they were busy for quite some time, before they returned to sleep.

AEFRIC WAS AWAKENED SOMETIME LATER BY OCTAVE'S GENTLE HAND. Though as his eyes opened, he was disappointed to see that she was already out of bed and dressed in her pale blue frock. That could only mean that their time together was coming to its end.

Morning light streamed in through the open windows, which said further that she'd been awake longer than she needed to be, just to slip into her dress.

All the same, Aefric was tempted to pull her back into bed. Not necessarily even to seek the bliss moment again — though she did make the prospect tempting — but just because he wasn't ready to start his day yet.

She must've seen the temptation in his eyes. She laughed joyously.

"Ah, would that I could slip back out of my dress and between those sheets with your grace again. But I have my duties to see to. And her lordship expects your grace to join her for the ride south to Asarchai, for the feast."

Aefric sighed.

"If it helps, your grace, Ser Beornric awaits you in the sitting room. With breakfast."

"Hardly a winning comparison," Aefric said, looking her over with a smile. "But I suppose it's time."

"Your grace should come just to visit sometime," Octave said. "Spend a few days here with no great agenda, and free to pursue ... other pastimes."

Aefric chuckled. "Temptress."

"Thank you, your grace," she said, looking pleased.

Aefric stretched and got out of bed, and was gratified that the sight of his naked form distracted Octave from whatever she intended to say next.

He stretched again, arms wide, legs tensed, and torso bowed with the move. Putting on a little show for her.

Octave stopped moving about and watched with frank approval.

"Perhaps your grace could visit again soon?" she asked, her voice a little huskier.

"I suspect I'll want to stop here for the night on my way back to Water's End."

"And I'll beg her lordship for the chance to offer your grace *leaba* when you do." She shook herself. "Come now, your grace. I cannot see to my other duties until you're washed and dressed."

"I can see to those things myself," Aefric said. "Wouldn't want you to get into trouble."

"Oh no, your grace," Octave said, smiling. "Can't have that. Not when these are the duties I'm most looking forward to today."

She took her time washing and shaving him at the copper basin, and afterward seemed to be groping him with the towels as much as drying him off.

But then she dressed Aefric in his brown riding leathers, with a silk tunic of navy blue, which had the Deepwater sigil — a lake, with a sword emerging from it hilt-first — embroidered in gold thread above his heart.

And she went out of her way to make sure she was satisfied with the way the fabric lay against his skin.

His boots for the day had hard soles, for traveling, but otherwise were of soft, buttery brown calfskin that cradled his feet and calves. His belt matched, and bore his belt pouch along with the sheaths of the wand Garram and his noble's dagger.

All nobles of Armyr wore a dagger at all times, no matter how formal the setting or complicated the outfit. A tradition that went back hundreds of years. Perhaps further.

This excellent dagger had been found for him in his new castle in Kivash. It had an ebony handle, carved with the likeness of a raven. A straight, steel blade edged in silver, about as long as Aefric's hand.

Octave then combed out Aefric's long, sandy blonde hair. Stroked his shoulders, back, and chest a few more times under the pretense of "dusting."

Finally, she stepped in front of him, looked him up and down critically, and said, "There. A proper noble. Or did your grace want to wear one of the hats I found in his trunk?"

Aefric chuckled. Hats had been out of fashion for a number of years in Armyr. But his valets at Water's End, especially Dajen, had been encouraging Aefric to wear hats, and make them fashionable again.

Both his valets seemed convinced that Aefric could somehow set the trend.

Of course, Aefric *would* be riding all day in the sun anyway...

"Perhaps a hat would help with the sun."

"Oh," Octave said, sounding more excited about the prospect than Aefric felt. "Then this one, your grace."

She went into the trunk and pulled out a bycocket hat. Its body was Deepwater gray, but its turned-back brim — which formed a point in front — was navy blue.

The hat also featured a colorful tailfeather from a pyltenius bird: a hint of yellow near the quill, through an orange that darkened into a blazing red and finally a deep blue at the tips.

She positioned the hat on Aefric's head. She put one hand to her chin and tilted her head one way and then the other, assessing the hat's position. She adjusted it slightly, then smiled.

"There. Perfect. The very image of Maddox himself."

Maddox. The name sounded vaguely familiar to old memories he had as Keifer, but Aefric didn't know the name at all.

"Maddox?"

"Your grace doesn't know the stories of Maddox?" Octave sounded scandalized. "An ancient wandering skald, solving problems and satisfying women everywhere he went." She smirked. "So the resemblance extends beyond the physical."

Aefric laughed. "Perhaps another hat would be more appropriate for a duke, then."

"No, please, your grace," Octave implored. "I tease, but the hat is most becoming. Please wear it."

"Very well," Aefric said.

"Thank you, your grace," Octave said with a bow. "And now, I should be about my duties."

"Wait," Aefric said, taking her by the shoulder as she turned away. Octave turned back, curious.

"I am, after all, permitted to give a present to the woman who offers me *leaba*."

Gifts were allowed, though not required. And nothing that could be construed as payment. So nothing in the way of coin, of course, or anything *too* valuable.

But Aefric had taken to carrying things he could give as gifts for such occasions.

In Kivash, where Duchess Ashling had permitted *two* women to offer him *leaba* together on each of three straight nights, he'd thrilled them with beautiful ivory combs.

Apparently they hadn't expected anything more than his company.

The first time Octave had given him *leaba*, he'd given her a bolt of fine cloth that matched the blue of her eyes.

This time, he'd brought something more personal, just in case she came to him again.

Aefric dug in the second large, wooden trunk for his old adventuring backpack. A massive, leather thing, strewn with more pockets than most would ever need, which meant *almost* enough pockets to suit him.

From within a small pocket sewn inside the main, central pouch of the backpack, he retrieved a simple, thin gold chain, with a faceted, teardrop crystal of purple rubellite.

Not what Andi had given him, of course. The links of that chain had been finer still, and the crystal had been quartz.

But the reference was obvious.

"Oh, your grace," Octave said, sounding astonished. "I couldn't. It's too fine. And—"

"There is symmetry between this and another necklace," Aefric said. "The woman who gave me the other necklace, I loved her more than life itself. After she died, I thought I would never hold another woman again. Never ... do a lot of things again."

He held up the gold chain with its rubellite.

"Fitting," he said, "that *this* necklace goes to the woman who reminded me that *I* am not dead. And that the woman whom I loved so fiercely would want to see me happy again. Would want to see me ... seek love with women again. Seek pleasure, with women again."

Aefric held the necklace up in both hands, and Octave, eyes misty and lips trembling, leaned forward so he could put it around her neck.

Once it was in place, he kissed her gently.

"Thank you, Octave. For everything."

"I promise you, your grace," Octave said, looking him in the eye, "the honor and the pleasure were mine."

The sitting room in Aefric's guest chambers at Norrtarr was small, but sufficient for its task. Gray stone walls, lightened with tapestries heavy on the pale yellows and blues.

The stone floor was covered in carpets woven from some kind of green leaves, strong as linen. A fresh, herbal scent to the air suggested that sweet herbs had been scattered beneath those carpets just yesterday.

Wide windows with their casements thrown open for a view past the farmland to the conifers of mighty Kerrik Forest in the distance to the east. Resplendent, with the sun only just cresting the tallest of those trees.

And before that window, a round oak table spread with an assortment of sliced meats and fruits, along with honeyed oat bread, a pair of copper mugs, and a copper ewer that Aefric knew would be filled with water. The traditional Armyrian breakfast drink, to go with the traditional Armyrian breakfast.

Two matching oak chairs at that table, large enough and strong enough to accommodate even Beornric, a man thick mostly with muscle, who quickly hopped to his feet as Aefric entered the room.

Ser Beornric Ol'Sandallas. A knight of strong reputation, from an old Armyrian noble family. He'd served directly under King Colm most of his twoscore and more summers, most notably during the Godswalk Wars.

But it was during the Godswalk Wars that Aefric's decisive actions at the Battle of Deepwater turned the tide against the armies of borogs marching in service to that evil god, Xazik the Flayer.

Aefric was called the Hero of Deepwater after that. And many credited him with saving countless lives.

As soon as Aefric was created Duke of Deepwater by King Colm Stronghand, Ser Beornric entered into Aefric's service. It didn't take him long to prove his worth and be named captain of Aefric's new Knights of the Lake, as well as a trusted adviser.

Beornric kept his graying black hair cut battlefield short, but since he'd come into Aefric's service, he'd grown out a bushy mustache that he seemed to enjoy quite a bit.

All knights had their scars, but Beornric's — from what Aefric has seen — were mostly on his hands and arms. Those scars on his arms were covered today by a quilted tunic of deep blood red, worn over brown riding leathers.

As always, his heavy longsword hung at his side.

"Good morning, your grace," Ser Beornric said with a smile. "I like the hat. Gives you a roguish look. Rather like Maddox."

"Good morning, Beornric," Aefric said. "I'll have to hear the stories of this Maddox sometime."

Aefric felt pleased with himself that he hadn't added the "ser" courtesy to Beornric's greeting. Beornric, along with Aefric's general, Ser Yrsa, had been working to break him of the habit of giving people their courtesies at all times, and instead doing so only when socially appropriate.

Tricky habit to break, it seemed.

Beornric chuckled as Aefric stood the Brightstaff beside his chair, and sat.

"That will take a good while," Beornric said. "Maddox's name is attached to a great many stories. I've always favored the tale of how he avoided a war by getting two tarok princesses to fight over him."

"I don't think taroks have princesses," Aefric said, selecting a slice of roast turkey. "Their governing style tends to be clan-based, with chiefs and subchiefs."

"Good story though," Beornric said with a shrug.

Aefric frowned as he chewed his first smoky bite of turkey. Cocked his head to one side.

"How did getting two princesses to fight over him *avert* a war?" he asked. "Seems to me like the sort of thing that *causes* wars."

Beornric smiled and stroked his mustaches.

"Would your grace care to hear the story? And delay discussing business?"

"No," Aefric said with a sigh. "I'm sure we have important matters to cover before we ride south with Baroness Herewyn. Any word from Yrsa?"

"A rika this morning from Ajenmoor. No signs of Malimfari ships anywhere near our waters. And no word about the pirate queen Nelazzi being anywhere near our coast. Some stirrings that she's west of the Risen Sea right now."

"Good. I take it the message was too short for word about our defenses, or our progress on rebuilding the coast?"

Most of Deepwater's coastal towns had been destroyed during the Godswalk Wars. Aefric hoped to have them at least partially rebuilt before winter.

"Not from Yrsa, but Baron Osmaer of Haven sends word that Haven's coastal towns are rebuilt, as are the three southernmost in your ducal lands. Osmaer continues his ride up the coast, seeing to the farmland while workers see to the towns and farms."

"Very good," Aefric said. "And I think his acolytes of the Green Lord... Well, I suppose they're full clerics themselves now ... they're all three in Goldenfall?"

The county of Goldenfall, the part of Deepwater most devastated by the Godswalk Wars.

"Not quite," Beornric said. "Two are in Goldenfall. The third is finishing her work in Felspark."

The barony west of Norra. Hit almost as hard as Goldenfall, though not quite.

"Good. I don't want any of my people starving come winter. Bad enough that many still lack their own homes." Aefric tossed three ripe, delicious slices of orange into his mouth, chewed them and swallowed before asking, "Any word from Kivash?"

Kivash. Coastal city on the southern bank of the Indecisive River, which formed the border between Armyr and Malimfar.

The city was once Malimfar's, but after Aefric stopped the Malimfari invasion at the Battle of Frozen Ridge — which Aefric still didn't think of as a *battle*, properly speaking — Armyr marched down the river valley and seized Kivash, in retribution.

Aefric had been given a castle there, as a sort of thank-you.

"Karbin remains there at Castle Cairdeas, working on those wards that Larus Hrafntonn left on your new grimoires. Apparently they're quite intricate. Though he says negotiations are near completion for returning those historical objects to the Hrafntonn family."

Aefric hadn't wanted any negotiations there. The Hrafntonn family had been forced to abandon a sort of family museum when they fled the castle he was later given. Old armor and weapons and artwork of far greater sentimental value than monetary.

Aefric had wanted to simply return those pieces of Hrafntonn family history as a gesture of goodwill.

But apparently that wasn't how things were done between noble families. The castle was now Aefric's, including everything within its walls.

Giving the Hrafntonn family back anything Aefric had inherited with the castle would be an insult. However, he had the option to *ransom* back any possessions he didn't want.

Part of the reason for all those layers of wards on the grimoires that Larus Hrafntonn had been forced to abandon. The Hrafntonn family wizard had been trying to force Aefric to ransom them back…

"Wait," Aefric said with a frown. "*Karbin* thinks those wards are intricate? He actually said that? 'Intricate' was the word *he* chose?"

Karbin was Aefric's ducal wizard, but also his oldest friend, and one of the finest magic-users he'd ever known.

It was Karbin who'd first recognized Aefric's talent for magic, back when Aefric was just a street rat in Sartis. Karbin, who'd begun training Aefric as a wizard.

And Karbin who'd been the first to realize that Aefric could go only so far as a wizard, for he was in truth the first dweomerblood…

"Yes," Beornric said, leaning a little closer across the table and tearing a slice of roast beef in half. "*Karbin* thinks those wards are intricate. So much so that the Feast of Dereth Sehk might pass before he feels ready to disarm even the first of them."

Aefric shook his head as he cut free a chunk of honeyed oat bread, and slathered it with butter.

"Did I warn Karbin about Hrafntonn's skill at illusion?"

"You did, your grace," Beornric said, wrapping a slice of roast beef around smaller slices of orange, nava, and apple.

Aefric shook his head. "That's got to be what's slowing him down, though. Hrafntonn must've wrapped illusions in his wards in clever ways. But how did he have time?"

"A question I'm sure Karbin will puzzle out," Beornric said, one wild eyebrow high. "And I'm equally sure that he does not need his duke to return to Kivash to aid him."

Aefric chuckled. "Don't worry. I wasn't going to abandon my duties and insult my court wizard just to solve a puzzle. No matter how tempting the puzzle."

A knock at the door was followed by Ser Wardius poking his head in.

Tough, wiry Wardius had the dubious distinction of being the most scarred knight Aefric knew. The man had jagged scars on both cheeks, and had lost the tip of his nose and the small finger of his left hand.

In fact, his hands showed more white scars than tanned skin. Only visible because he had yet to don his gauntlets. Otherwise Wardius, as one of Aefric's Knights of the Lake, was clad in his full plate armor, with its breastplate etched in an image of Lake Deepwater.

"Your grace," Wardius said, "the servants are here for your luggage."

Aefric waved for them to come in.

"We better hurry up and eat," Beornric said. "It's a long road to Asarchai."

"No it isn't," Aefric said. "We'll be there by mid-afternoon."

"Well, it's a long road on an empty stomach."

"Good point," Aefric said with a laugh. And together, they tucked into their breakfast.

Even properly fed, Aefric found that the road to Asarchai felt longer than it should have. Especially considering that the wide road was covered in smooth, level slats of seamless pale granite. Very easy for walking or riding.

But then, Aefric had a lifetime of calibration to overcome, when it came to travel times.

When Aefric was an adventurer — whether traveling alone or with a small band of companions — he had three speeds: meandering, standard, and urgent.

While meandering, the road from Norrtarr to Asarchai — which was almost as broad as the Kingsroad, and, thanks to the granite, even better maintained — would have taken all day.

He would have lingered, enjoying the smell of ripening wheat on the warm summer air. He'd have taken long breaks everywhere the farmers kept roadside stands selling fresh fruits and vegetables. Even napped, in the shade of a copse of oak and beech trees.

At his standard pace, he would have reached Asarchai before midday. Of course, in those days, he would have left right about dawn.

But even considering the later hour of his departure that morning, at his old standard pace he'd likely have missed a midday arrival by no more than an hour.

The distance was short enough to push a horse safely. At least, the quality of horses he rode in those days. When he rode real horses. As opposed to his *magaunt* — a spell-summoned, phantasmal steed — which covered ground faster than any horse could, safely.

And when pressing need saw Aefric traveling at an urgent pace, he flew. He could only travel alone that way. He'd never worked out the issues inherent in extending flight to others. But, flying, he could have covered the distance between Norrtarr and Asarchai in perhaps an hour. Certainly not much more.

But Aefric was a duke now, and it seemed a duke generally traveled at a pace too quick to be called *meandering*, and certainly too slow to be called *urgent*.

No. It was clearly his new "standard" pace. It was just much slower than what Aefric was used to thinking of as his standard pace.

The difference, he suspected, came down to two things.

Appearances and numbers.

When traveling without a pressing need for speed, Aefric was expected to ride slowly enough that the local common folk could pause in their work to come and wave, as they watched their duke pass.

Not a mandatory, thing, of course. Still, Aefric rarely rode anywhere without a good number of people coming out to cheer him, or yell out wishes for his long life, and the like.

That bright morning, many of the local farm workers even approached the road to throw flowers and call out blessings on Aefric and Baroness Herewyn.

Apparently the locals were happy with the progress being made in recovering after the Godswalk Wars.

The flowers were orange honeysuckle. And they smelled as nice as they looked.

Honeysuckle. Maev's scent. An association that made Aefric smile wistfully, at the thought of the beautiful princess. Would that she were here now, and not off in Varondam…

Distracting himself from that melancholy line of thought, it occurred to Aefric that riding slowly could be construed as a show of power, in places where he might not be so well-loved. After all, he hardly rode alone.

Which brought him to the numbers factor.

Only his brief time riding with the royal entourage a few aetts back had meant riding with a larger group of people than he rode with that late summer day.

Beornric rode at his right hand, of course, and Aefric's six other

Knights of the Lake, resplendent in their full plate armor, rode guard before, behind, and to both sides.

To Aefric's immediate left rode her lordship Herewyn Ol'Norette, Baroness of Norra.

The baroness was a beautiful woman. And not just in her smooth skin — which was fashionably pale — her bright green eyes, or her long, shimmering red hair, which today was bound back into braids for the ride.

Hers was one of the oldest noble families in Armyr, and it showed. Perhaps five years older than Aefric — which would make her about a decade into her majority — she had the kind of grace and poise that commanded rooms easily.

Today she wore a silk tunic the color of the midsummer sky, cut to flatter her figure well, over well-worn brown riding leathers.

At her side, a rapier that looked to be more than mere ornament.

To Herewyn's left rode Sighild Ol'Masarkor, heir to a barony in the county of Fyretti, and a beauty in her own right.

Aefric knew that Sighild was Herewyn's cousin — and younger by about a decade — but looked more like her younger sister. Same shimmering hair — Sighild's was longer, and hung past her waist when not bound in braids and ribbons as it was that day — and same bright green eyes.

Though Sighild's eyes had small flecks of gold that shined when she smiled. And her skin, a slight dusting of freckles.

But then, Aefric had spent more time with Sighild. She was one of the contenders to be his duchess.

Sighild wore a cream-colored silk tunic over her brown riding leathers. And her rapier didn't look as well-used.

The four of them formed the nucleus of this massive riding party.

More than forty knights, perhaps half of whom owed their fealty directly to Aefric, including Ser Beornric and the Knights of the Lake.

Perhaps a hundred soldiers, two dozen of whom were part of Aefric's personal guard. The rest were Herewyn's.

Another reason a duke had to travel so slowly. All those soldiers marched. They didn't ride. Or at least, they weren't riding that day.

And since perhaps a quarter of them preceded the group's nucleus, the horses — even walking — couldn't go faster than the slowest foot soldier.

And then there was the entourage trailing along behind.

No servants, for this trip. Not coming down for work, anyway. Herewyn kept a small keep at Asarchai, which she said held more than enough staff.

But there were still hundreds of people following in Aefric's wake.

Petty nobles and landed knights, with their own entourages, coming down from the area around Norrtarr for the celebration.

Farmers, traders, merchants and crafters, all with goods to sell, for the feast would also provide one of the five grandest markets Norra would see all year, and the last before the great harvest festival in the coming season.

And others, who could take time away from their work to simply come enjoy the festivities.

Yes, no one traveling with a company as large as this one could do so quickly.

Still, the road was wide, and smooth. So though the pace may have been slow, progress was steady.

And the company was good. As they rode through the late morning and into the early afternoon, Herewyn told stories of various sites they passed. Sighild sang old Norran songs. Aefric told of more recent events down in Kivash — mostly about the efforts involved in subduing his new castle — and Beornric told of gossip from Armyr's capital, Armityr, that had been passed to him by various relatives.

In all, it was a pleasant ride until Aefric asked the wrong question.

"Are you expecting any other members of the ranking nobility?"

"Alas," Herewyn said in her smoky contralto. "Baroness Blaewyn won't be coming over from Felspark this year." Herewyn shook her head sadly. "A pity. The Feast is one of our few chances to get together without worrying at each other over trade and border issues."

"Border issues?" Aefric asked. "Anything I should be aware of?"

"Nothing worth bothering your grace," Herewyn said with a

dismissive gesture. "Small details that our families have squabbled over for generations. Not exactly a cause to take up arms."

That phrasing wasn't very reassuring, but he decided not to push.

"What keeps her away?" Aefric asked. "Recovery matters?"

"Just so," Herewyn said. "Though those clerics of the Green Lord you sent did wonders, she still has a great deal to organize before the rains return in earnest."

"Countess Faenella won't be able to attend either," Sighild said. "She's enmeshed in trade matters."

Faenella was Fyretti's countess, and Sighild's direct liege lord.

"That's too bad," Aefric said. "I haven't seen either of them in too long. And I know Osmaer is too busy along the coast to attend. Any word from Goldenfall or Riverbreak?"

"Goldenfall is busier than Felspark," Beornric said. "And Count Cyneric's health is failing, putting that much more burden on his son, Taeric."

"I understand that Taeric's sister, Riverbreak's Baroness Regent, Byrhta Ol'Caran, won't be attending for the same reason," Herewyn said. "I believe she's returning to Goldenfall to see to her father."

Odd. Byrhta had said nothing of this in her most recent letter to Aefric, which he'd received not three days past. And Byrhta wouldn't withhold something like that. She'd been looking forward to seeing Aefric as much as he'd been looking forward to seeing her.

She was, after all, one of the leading contenders for Aefric's hand.

"There will be at least one other titled noble arriving, though," Herewyn said, sounding not altogether pleased. "Count Ferrin of Motte has sent word that he'll attend."

Of course. The only one of Aefric's titled vassals who'd be traveling in for the feast was also the only one he didn't want to see.

Count Ferrin. The obnoxious fop who'd conspired against Aefric, threatened him with force, and then had the gall to complain when Aefric punished him for these things.

So much for Aefric's hope that the feast would be a bit of a vacation…

2

Asarchai was a type of town that Aefric had never seen before, even in all his travels. Here in Qorunn, there might not even be a term for it.

But it was a type of town that the part of him that had grown up on Earth recognized immediately.

Asarchai was a tourist town.

It sprawled lazily on both sides of the wide, slow Fyrsa River, but without interfering with the main road, which continued on south. Likely to Norra's quarries, the source of the granite slats on that road.

A town surrounded by no more than a handful of farms. With broad fields dedicated to camping. Those fields closer to town already had dozens of pavilions in place. While further afield, those without pavilions pitched tents, or gathered sleeping rolls around fires, or even slept in their carts, in some cases.

Inns and taverns outnumbered every other business in Asarchai by a fair stretch.

Stranger still, especially for a fairly small town, there had to be at least three or four large, stone theaters. Enclosed buildings, as opposed to the additional half-dozen open-air theaters.

Already Aefric could smell dozens of cook fires, roasting meats and baking breads. Not to mention the distinctive smell of a large number of horses. Many more even than rode with Aefric's long train of travelers.

He could hear a great many hammers — driving stakes, working steel, and erecting stands and booths out among the fields. He could hear waves of conversation cresting and breaking against one another, with occasional shouts and laughter and crashes of one kind or another.

And past it all, near the far edge of town, stood a coliseum. A rarity even among cities, much less a small town like this one. Water's End and Ajenmoor were both several times as large as Asarchai, but neither of those cities boasted a coliseum.

Aefric hadn't even seen one since … Sartis? No. Goldenmoon. Perhaps three or four years past.

This coliseum loomed out at the eastern edge of town, near the river. It stood even taller than Herewyn's keep, which sat in the center of town.

Hard to judge exactly how large it was, that coliseum. At least, from where Aefric approached Asarchai, along the road. But it looked like a giant made of granite, squatting down for a closer look at the small town.

"Ah," Herewyn said with a smile. "I see you've spotted the Teryrnon Grand Theater. Named for the ancestor who commissioned it, some … four centuries ago, I believe."

"Four centuries?" Aefric asked, surprised. Such a feat would have been beyond most builders, unless…

"Ah," he said, understanding. "Your family has been employing *vohlcairns* a long time."

"Very good, your grace," Herewyn said, smiling, while Sighild beamed beside her. "We find *vohlcairns* to be the most practical choice for court wizards. Little help with intrigue, of course, but excellent at so many other things."

"She must come down here to maintain it…"

"About every fourth or fifth aett," Herewyn said, "depending on the season. Though I believe one of her apprentices is finally competent enough to handle the maintenance."

"How many apprentices does she have?"

"Three, this time," Herewyn said, frowning. "Her fourth crop, and none of the rest have been satisfactory. But I don't need to tell your grace how difficult it is to train a wizard. Let alone a specialist."

It was true. Magic was the most powerful force in Qorunn, but it was also the hardest to tame.

Some were born to it, such as the dweomerblades. And Aefric, of course.

Some gained it through prayer and divine guidance, such as clerics, shamans, and the Order of Blessed Knights. Though prayer and devotion were not enough. The gods had to take a liking to the petitioner, or all the prayer in the world wouldn't garner more than silence in return.

And the gods bestowed such favor on few.

Others, such as warlocks ... made deals with lesser powers. Though that did not diminish their potency in this world.

In theory, their numbers could be legion. Certainly the lesser powers stood always ready to deal.

But few were those desperate enough, or driven enough, to take those deals.

Finally, there were the wizards.

The common view was that all a wizard needed was a good mind, and enough devotion to study.

But that wasn't the case. One needed the *right* kind of mind to become a wizard. Intellectual enough to handle the complexity of arcane study, yes, but artistic enough to see beyond the logic to the beauty inherent in spellwork.

Still, one could have both those qualities and fail to complete apprenticeship. Because one had to have the *will* to channel those immense arcane forces and submit them to one's needs.

Yes, it was the nature of magical work that kept Qorunn's magic-users few in number, no matter how many aspirants tried each year to join their ranks.

But doubtless among the throngs at the Feast would be some of those failed magic-users, performing such small tricks and "miracles" as they could, to earn their living.

Those failures called themselves "magicians." Among the magic-using community, though, they were known as "sparkers." Because if magic was fire, they could do nothing more than spark.

"Sparkers" was a fairly recent term though, and much more polite than the older term — "hacks."

As his cavalcade turned down Asarchai's main street, Aefric could see one such sparker. A bent old graybeard in fraying robes, who nonetheless held a small crowd's rapt attention by punctuating a scary story he told with ghostly wolf howls, and distant-sounding cries.

Those sounds were the sort of simple illusion work Aefric had learned in the earliest days of his apprenticeship. But they were still more magic than most common folk would encounter.

This street here was cobbled — likely stones from the nearby river — but even wider than the granite road. Likely built that way to accommodate the sort of crowds that the Feast would draw.

More mouth-watering smells filled the air. Juicy meats, roasting or frying. Cinnamon sugared treats. At least four kinds of berry pies that Aefric could pick out. And the smells of beer and ale were already making themselves known.

Strangely, there were no vendors set up along the street though. He turned to ask Herewyn, but she must've seen the question in his eyes.

"They're not allowed to set up stalls until the morning of the first day of the Feast, and merchants, traders and peddlers only. Never food stalls along this street. A little law to help the permanent establishments. After all, who'd go all the way into a tavern to eat, if fifteen different food stalls were closer?"

"Fair enough," Aefric said.

"Believe me, though," Herewyn said with a smile. "It's a law that gets argued before the town council every year. But the mayor manages to keep it in place all the same."

"It's the farmers versus the townsfolk," Sighild said, "and the townsfolk have them outnumbered."

Aefric frowned. "So during the feast, the farmers want to sell directly to the travelers, rather than selling to the inns and taverns?"

"The farmers tried raising their prices during the Feast," Herewyn said, "but it didn't work. The farms around Norrtarr are too close. The inns and taverns threatened to import all their food."

"Bet that went over well," Aefric said.

Just looking around he could already see over a dozen different inns and taverns on this street alone. Many of them two-story. A couple of them even three-story.

And they were all finely tooled. Freshly scrubbed stone and wood fronts. Clear, recently refurbished signs. And even though it was only mid-afternoon, every one of them was already raucous with business.

Mixed in among the inns, taverns, and shop fronts, the occasional theater. Though those were not yet open and doing business.

"The two factions almost came to blows," Herewyn said. "Weapons were drawn. The town watch had to separate them."

"There were arrests, weren't there?" Sighild asked.

"A few, but only overnight," Herewyn said. "Mostly giving certain people a chance to cool their heads."

"How did they resolve it?" Aefric asked.

"The mayor finally met with the leaders of both factions," Herewyn said. "Acted as an intermediary, negotiating terms. They agreed that the farmers couldn't raise prices during festival seasons, but they *could* set up their own stalls to sell food directly to travelers."

Aefric chuckled, as they passed groups of people — humans mostly, but a few eldrani and kindaren — with quantities of lumber, who looked to be staking out locations for the stalls they couldn't set up yet.

"Let me guess," he said. "They made this agreement, and it lasted exactly one festival before the owners of those inns and taverns complained about the food stalls on this street cutting down their custom?"

"Didn't take that long," Herewyn said. "They came to terms before the Midsummer Festival ... perhaps a decade ago. And by the end of the first day, the owners of the inns and taverns were screaming about lost business, and the town council had to take immediate action."

"You'd go mad," Beornric said, "trying to keep everyone happy."

Herewyn shrugged, and somehow made it look like a dance move.

"Asarchai makes more money during any one festival than it does during all the non-festival parts of the year combined," she said. "And right now, all of its people are prospering. The farmers might complain about wanting to make more money, but it's a tough sell while everyone's doing well."

There were no trees along the main street, which struck Aefric as strange, until he decided that they must want every available yard of space for either tourists, or stalls.

They reached the spacious town square then, which was anchored at the corners by four huge structures.

Two of them were large stonework theaters. Big enough to seat more than a hundred patrons, easily. One was an even larger open-air theater, where workers were buzzing around, getting everything ready for tomorrow.

The fourth, sitting behind a ten-foot tall, smooth granite wall, stood Herewyn's keep.

HEREWYN'S KEEP AT ASARCHAI WAS A WIDE TOWER, FOUR STORIES TALL. It was made entirely of smooth, pale granite, flecked with darker colors, with a crenellated top.

Even over the ten-foot wall — made from that same, seamlessly smooth, pale granite — Aefric could see that each of the floors had wide, arched windows, providing an excellent view in all directions.

Herewyn gave Aefric a coquettish smile as they approached the broad granite gates.

"No need to ask, your grace," she said. "It was my father who commissioned this keep, and paid *Vohlcairna* Burrew to build it as one of her first official acts as a full wizard, after graduating her apprenticeship."

"She built *that* as a new wizard?" Aefric asked, as his eyebrows tried to knock off his hat. "But it would have taken…"

"Building that keep took her all spring and summer, and partway into autumn," Herewyn said. "Our previous court wizard, *Vohlcairn* Karkasso, had been more than ready to retire, but hung on long enough to let her finish. He didn't want to leave us without a wizard at court."

Aefric nodded, looking over the towering keep again. No strong sense of magic to it, which meant that it had been designed according to sound architectural principals, rather than relying on magic to make up the difference.

Of course, from here, it looked like a simple enough structure. Solid. Wide. Round. Not even a hint of damage from the wars…

"She's always been thorough," Herewyn said. "Even among *vohlcairns*. She designed the structure herself. Its so solid it doesn't even require maintenance."

"You *can't* tell me that's true about a granite gate," Aefric said, as the cavalcade came to a halt just outside the gates. And even without trying he could feel a hint of magic about them.

Herewyn's smile stretched into a grin. "It's a thin layer of granite over oak, actually. But spell-hardened stronger than steel." She nodded once, to Aefric. "And yes, your grace, it requires refreshing about once a season."

"That's still not much." Aefric shook his head. "Why haven't you implemented such things at your Norrtarr castle?"

"I was going to, but then the gods came down and ruined most of my long-term plans."

She frowned towards the front, where one of the soldiers who'd come down from Norrtarr with them was talking to one of the two chainmail-clad pikemen outside the gate.

"What's the holdup?" she asked. She didn't raise her voice, but her words still carried on the warm afternoon air.

The conversation at the gate wrapped up, and her soldier came trotting back with a grim look on his face. He bowed deeply to Herewyn and Aefric, but spoke only to her.

"We have ... unexpected guests at the keep, your lordship. The guards wanted you informed before entering the grounds, in case your lordship wanted to issue any orders."

"What unexpected guests?" Aefric asked. Hope flickered in his chest that Maev had returned from her mission to Varondam, and had come here to surprise him with good news.

Certainly the arrival of Armyr's princess would be enough to cause a stir...

Such thoughts distracted him, though, and he missed the soft reply from the soldier.

"Well," Herewyn said with a sigh, "consider me warned. I'll deal with him myself."

The official call came to open the gates, and though their hinges creaked a bit in protest, Aefric was impressed at how smoothly they opened. Considering their granite coating.

The grounds inside the wall were already more than half-full. People and horses and carts. Knights and soldiers, servants and more.

A half dozen pennants flying, and chief among them...

... the black bull, rampant, facing to the dexter on a background of purple.

The flag of the county of Motte.

Count Ferrin Ol'Nylla had arrived early, it seemed.

Herewyn made a series of gestures with her left hand. Battlefield signals, unless Aefric was mistaken.

Bowmen on the walls nodded acknowledgment.

A half dozen of her knights approached on horseback from further back in the procession, along the left flank of the procession.

Herewyn turned to Aefric.

"There seems to be a misunderstanding in the mind of Count Ferrin regarding accommodations for the Feast. I should only require a moment to straighten this out, if your grace would not mind waiting."

"Not at all," Aefric said. "In fact, if it would help, I would be happy to accompany you."

"Your grace is most kind to offer," Herewyn said. "But I can handle Ferrin."

"To be clear," Aefric said, as Herewyn began turning away. He waited until she looked back at him, curiosity in her bright green eyes, before continuing. "I never doubted that. I only wanted to watch the show."

Whatever Herewyn was expecting Aefric to say, it wasn't that. Surprised laughter burst out of her, and she covered her mouth with one hand.

"I find your grace's frank humor most appealing," she said with a smile that put a small frown on her cousin's face. "But I suspect this will go more smoothly if your grace remains out here."

"I don't think there's any doubting that," Beornric said with a rough chuckle. "Ferrin would take one look at his grace and set his feet."

"By all means then," Aefric said, with a wave of his hand telling her to proceed. "Far be it for me to make your life harder."

That got him another quick smile, before Herewyn moved off to join her knights and ride past the gates.

Once she was gone, Aefric said, "Ferrin *was* expected, I thought."

"Expected at the *Feast*, yes," Sighild said, steering her horse a few steps closer. "But not at the keep." She shook her head. "Last year, while he sat Duke Regent in Deepwater, Prince Killian attended the Feast, but declined hospitality in favor of renting out a pair of inns for himself and his entourage."

"Ah," Aefric said, understanding. "So that made room in the keep for Ferrin?"

"It did," Sighild said, and frowned. "He shouldn't have expected your grace to do the same, though. His highness spent much of his time as regent finding ways to put more money into Deepwater's economy."

"His father kept him out of much of the Godswalk Wars," Beornric said softly. "Didn't want to risk his heir on the battlefield. I suspect Prince Killian felt guilty about that. Wanted to make it up to those who suffered, where he could."

Aefric could believe that. He'd only met Prince Killian briefly, but he seemed a good man.

The conversation in the courtyard stretched on longer than expected. The knights and soldiers in the cavalcade began to grow restless.

The smells of food seemed more enticing now. Lunch had been hours ago. And the sounds of work seemed sharper, easily drowning out whatever was being said in the courtyard.

As Aefric looked ahead to the gates once more, he noticed that most of the archers on the walls were watching the courtyard, not their surroundings. And many of them kept one hand near their arrows...

"Think she's expecting trouble?" Aefric asked softly.

He'd been asking Beornric, but Sighild answered.

"I believe your grace knows that Count Ferrin ... has something of a bellicose nature," she said quietly. "Any time he comes with swords backing him up, my cousin has a tendency to keep her people ready. Just in case."

"I will not let this come to blows," Aefric said. "Maybe I *should* head in there."

"No, your grace," Beornric stage whispered.

"Please desist, your grace," Sighild implored, reaching out to grab Aefric's hand on the reins. "Herewyn knows what she's doing."

Someone spoke loudly in the courtyard. A man. Possibly Count Ferrin. But Aefric lost the details behind the nearby work sounds. Stalls might not have been allowed on the main street today, but they were clearly allowed on the side streets. Because they were being assembled at a quick pace.

A shout now. A woman's voice, but not Herewyn's. Aefric picked out the word *dare*...

He fought down a strong urge to ride ahead.

"Beornric," Aefric said.

"Your grace?"

"Would it be out of bounds for me to send you ahead to ask about the holdup?"

"I shouldn't think so, your grace."

"Sighild," Aefric said, "would your cousin take that as an insult?"

"I don't believe so, your grace."

Aefric nodded at Beornric.

Beornric began to spur his horse forward.

Trumpets sounded out loudly, somewhere behind them.

BAD ENOUGH THAT AEFRIC WAS STILL SITTING HIS HORSE IN THE MIDDLE of the cobbled Asarchai town square, waiting for Herewyn to explain to Ferrin that he and his rather large entourage would have to seek accommodations elsewhere.

Bad enough that, even though this was the fourth day before autumn, the afternoon was growing overwarm.

Though, admittedly, that might've just been impatience on Aefric's part. He was done with traveling for the day. He wanted to dismount. See his rooms. Clean up a little after the long day's ride.

Funny, that Beornric had called the road to Asarchai long. That morning, in Norrtarr, it hadn't looked long. No more than three-fourths of a day's ride, even as part of a huge cavalcade.

But now that Aefric was here — and having to wait yet longer before he could actually *arrive* — the day was wearing on him even more than than the bright sun.

Didn't help that he could smell those juicy roasting meats and frying bacon, baking breads and pies and cakes.

His stomach growled reminders that his lunch of roast chicken with crisp, ripe pears seemed a lifetime ago.

No, all of that was bad enough.

Now he could hear a trumpet announcing the arrival of ... well, someone important enough to merit trumpeting their arrival. Aefric was still new enough to his title that he couldn't pick out the different fanfares.

He could recognize his own, and the royal fanfare. The one he heard now was neither.

And what that really meant was that all of his and Herewyn's knights and soldiers and other retainers were clogging the main street, while some other titled noble was trying to get through.

An actual traffic jam, here in Asarchai. He thought he'd left those behind on Earth.

Beornric, who'd been about to ride into the courtyard of the keep and see what was holding up the discussion between Count Ferrin and Baroness Herewyn, turned back to Aefric, the question plain on his face.

"Go ahead," Aefric said with a nod.

Beornric frowned through his thick mustache, but spurred his horse past the remaining knights and soldiers, toward the courtyard of Herewyn's tower keep.

The Knights of the Lake closed ranks around Aefric. They didn't come in tight enough to get in his way, but they surrounded him and Sighild close enough to take an arrow, if needed.

Aefric looked back down the cavalcade. It was significantly smaller than earlier, when its ranks had been swelled by petty nobles and landed knights local to Norrtarr, as well as scores of common folk, traveling with the entourage for safety.

All of those people were gone now, of course. They'd departed at the fields set aside for tents and pavilions and other camping.

Nevertheless, the crowd behind Aefric was too big, and the wind too still, for him to spot a banner, let alone recognize one.

"Did you know that fanfare?" Aefric asked Sighild.

She shook her head. "Not royal, nor any noble from Deepwater."

"Not Merrek's, either," Ser Arras said, from the other side of Sighild. "Nor Silverlake's."

It was an unacknowledged truth that Arras was the bastard daughter of Deepwater's last duchess, Arinda Soulfist. And in Arras, Aefric could see the pale beauty that her mother must've had.

Though Arras kept her shining black hair cut battlefield short.

And her hazel eyes dared anyone to call her "pretty." At least, while she wore her full plate armor.

"A foreign noble then," Aefric said, nonplussed.

The Feast of Dereth Sehk wasn't really celebrated outside of Norra. At least, not that Aefric had heard. The other nobles of Deepwater were always invited, but Norra's barons were never offended by refusals.

So far as Aefric knew, no foreign nobles had ever attended. Though, really, he would need to ask Herewyn, to be certain.

Of course, if word had gotten out that Aefric would be attending, that might be enough to draw interest.

Malimfar and Caiperas had both sent princesses to meet him only a few aetts ago. And he'd received word that Rethneryl, Hatay and Shachan all might seek a marriage alliance with Aefric and Deepwater...

"Go back there and check it out," Aefric said to Arras. "Let whoever it is know that we've been delayed by a misunderstanding, and will clear the street presently. And find out who it is."

"Yes, your grace," Arras said with a small bow. She turned her horse and rode down along the side, past the other knights and soldiers, as well as the carts and wagons of Herewyn's other retainers.

Aefric was watching her ride off, when from the keep's courtyard came a very loud, "Ha!"

"That sounded like Ser Beornric," Sighild said, and Aefric nodded agreement.

Just what was Beornric doing in there?

The archers on the walls all had hands ready to draw arrows now, though none had gone so far as to nock.

Aefric shook his head. "They better not start a skirmish. Not with some foreign noble looking on..."

"It won't come to that, your grace," Sighild said, though the look in her eyes was troubled, and she sounded as though she were trying to convince herself.

And she betrayed another sign of nerves. Usually, whenever she had a few minutes alone with Aefric, she flirted. Ever since earlier in the summer, when she'd made known her intentions toward him.

Intentions buoyed by Queen Eppida, who has promised to see Sighild well dowered — perhaps even given a grander title than the barony she was heir to — if Aefric decided to marry her.

And Sighild had been much more open about her flirtations since Aefric first invited her to his rooms one night, a few aetts back.

But during this very delay, she'd grabbed Aefric's hand to implore him not to ride forward and investigate. And she'd withdrawn her hand without even giving his a squeeze first.

Now her eyes were locked on the half-closed gate. Though if she could see some sign of what was going on in the courtyard, she had better eyes than Aefric.

At last, though, the gates of the keep opened wide, and the first knights emerged, mounted, flying pennants bearing the sigil of Motte.

Following those knights, the whole of Ferrin's entourage, including the count himself, who seemed to go out of his way not to notice or acknowledge Aefric.

Ferrin's knights proceeded down a side street, possibly towards the campgrounds, to set up their pavilions.

Sighild gave Aefric a bright smile. "As I said, your grace. My cousin knows how to handle him."

Beornric came riding back.

"It's handled, your grace," he said, smiling. "Her lordship awaits you within, once his nibs gets his people out of the way."

"And just what was that 'Ha!' about?" Aefric asked.

"Oh, a small matter only, your grace," Beornric said, smiling broadly behind his mustache. "Nothing that should be of concern."

"Well," Aefric said, "if it's a *small* matter, then there should be no trouble—"

"Ser Arras returns," Sighild said, pointing back to where Ser Arras was, indeed, riding back along the outside of the train of horses, carts and people.

Aefric gave Sighild a suspicious look. The timing of her observation could have been construed as changing the subject...

A season ago, Aefric would have bought the innocence in her eyes, as she looked back at him. He knew her better now, though. Distraction had been entirely her goal here.

But why?

Either way, Arras rode up looking pale and slightly stricken.

Aefric sat straighter in his saddle to see such a look on so unflappable a knight, as did Beornric beside him. Aefric casually reached for the Brightstaff, where it sat in its sling attached to his saddle. He did not draw it forth yet, though.

Arras bowed in her saddle. "Your grace, behind us rides a woman identified to me as Princess Sorcha Diadiniu." She met Aefric's eyes. "Of Kefthal."

Kefthal.

There were only a few lands across Qorunn that Aefric thought of as *evil*. Chaotic Hayroun, controlled by its series of inconsistent, yet always warring factions.

Foul Zhenderran, with its reputation for dark, twisted rites — not all of which were tied to their gods.

Chief among these evil lands, though, was Kefthal. Oppressive Kefthal. Slave-ridden Kefthal. Ruled by...

"But Kefthal couldn't have a princess," Aefric said, frowning back at the stricken mien of Arras. "They have no monarch. They're ruled by the Nine Beyond Death."

The Nine Beyond Death. A council of necromancers. Possibly all liches. Rumors conflicted on that point, and if anyone living had ever seen them, Aefric didn't know about it.

Sighild made a small, nervous sound that drew his attention. Her green eyes were always large, but as she turned to Aefric then, they seemed almost to swallow her face.

"Kefthal?" she said, her voice steadier than her aspect. "Here?"

"So it seems," Aefric said, loudly, trying to suppress the sudden rush of conversation surrounding him from the lips of his Knights of the Lake.

Not that Aefric could blame them. Talk of Kefthal was for late nights around a campfire, not a bright, late summer day in a vibrant town square.

His knights grew quiet, to hear what Aefric said next. For a moment, the sounds of impatient horses and distant construction and revelry made the topic feel even stranger.

But rather than speaking, Aefric raised an eyebrow at Arras.

"I know little more than I have already spoken, your grace. Her herald gave her name as Sorcha Diadiniu, and Princess of Kefthal was the title attributed to her."

She grimaced. "I thought it imprudent to ask to see her patent of nobility."

Aefric snorted. "I quite agree." He turned to his knight-adviser. "What do you think?"

"This is the first I've heard of Kefthal claiming a princess," Beornric said. "But it is said that the Nine live like kings, dividing Kefthal among them. Perhaps she claims kinship with one."

Aefric considered that through a long, slow breath.

"Well," he said, "I cannot imagine why anyone would claim a title from Kefthal unless they had one. We'll have to treat her claim as valid for now, and send plenty of rikas, once we're inside Herewyn's tower."

"There remains one more matter, your grace," Arras said. "Princess Sorcha requests the honor of a 'quick word' while we're all stalled in the street."

"If we're not going to dispute her claim to be a princess..." Beornric cautioned.

Aefric sighed. "Then I can't very well refuse her. All right. I guess there's no harm in my talking to her."

"Not with your knights close at hand, no," Beornric said firmly.

Aefric chuckled. "I hadn't meant to go alone."

"Yrsa's not here," Beornric said with a smile. "And she asked me to make sure your grace—"

"Didn't do anything excessively stupid?"

"I don't believe she said 'excessively.'"

Aefric gave Beornric a droll look.

"Well," Beornric hedged, "your grace *has* encouraged her to speak her mind."

"Let's go," he said, then, almost as an afterthought added to Sighild. "Would you mind riding ahead, and informing Herewyn about all this?"

"Happily, your grace," Sighild said with a flirty smile that looked more normal for her.

Aefric and his Knights of the Lake moved outside the procession, then, and made their way back to the rear, where this so-called princess of Kefthal waited.

Necromancy was … an unusual art, even among the various types of Qorunn's magic. It seemed to manifest along several different, distinct paths.

There was necromancy involved in the way clerics would lay restless spirits to rest. In the ways shamans communicated with their ancestors.

Some even said that there was necromancy in the healing arts of the clerics of Nilasah herself. Though Aefric doubted that.

Aefric had felt both those other forms of necromancy before, as well as similar forms, and they'd all felt almost … warm. Heartening. Like some small reassurance that there were natural aspects to life beyond death and that their magics that could smooth the way.

But there were darker paths of necromancy of well. Spells that created hideous mockeries of life. Rites that bound the dead into service, or even tortured the very souls of the living.

Aefric's experience with those darker forms had been limited, but all too intense. He would never forget the common sensation such magics carried.

They all felt cold. Not the chill of crisp winter morning air, either, but the leeching freeze of soaking sea winds in the depth of winter that make warmth seem like a mere fever dream of the dying.

Aefric felt a whisper of that cold now, riding closer to this company said to be from Kefthal. And with that whisper, the undeniable sense of necromancy.

Perhaps this Princess Sorcha truly was from Kefthal?

Well, whoever she was, she traveled with two score knights. All clad in full plate armor of black steel. They wore bat winged helmets, all with their visors down.

Two enclosed carriages, made from ebony, but trimmed in gold and silver. Six enclosed wagons, made from a cheaper form of blackwood.

All eight drivers were dressed head to toe in black ... cotton, from the look of it. Cowls pulled down low, hiding their faces.

Their horses were impressive. Huge things that made the Keifer part of Aefric think of beer commercials. Though the Aefric part of him had seen such creatures ridden by some of the larger human warriors he'd known over the years.

Odd, though, that these supposedly Kefthali used such beasts both as warhorses and draft horses.

One rider stood out in the sea of black armor. A bald man in bloodred robes, embroidered with gold thread. His skin was bone white. Chalky. Lacking any hair at all, even eyebrows. And he smiled with too many teeth.

He wore two wands at his belt, and a greenwood staff rode in a sling beside his saddle, similar to the way Aefric carried the Brightstaff even now.

This bald man had the feel of a powerful wizard, holding his magic well in check. Interesting.

Aefric and his company stopped a reasonable distance back from the Kefthalis. Aefric's own soldiers stood nearby watching curiously, though holding ranks.

Less organized were a growing number of equally curious locals, who'd stopped their preparations and diversions to see what was unfolding.

Though at least the locals had the sense to stay well back. Perhaps, on some level, they too could feel the threat of that whisper of necromancy?

Beornric began the introductions.

"I have the honor to present his grace, Ser Aefric Brightstaff. Duke of Deepwater, Baron of Netar, Hero of the Battle of Deepwater, and Hero of the Battle of Frozen Ridge."

The full introduction raised a small swell of guilt in Aefric. He'd been given the barony of Netar aetts ago, but he'd yet to visit it...

The bald wizard's smile actually widened, displaying even more teeth. And every one of those teeth were the same shade as his skin.

Aefric had faced many disturbing things during his adventuring days. A series of shadows that twisted into oddly angled creatures that spoke only in creaking sounds. A tomb's echo that returned five times to pummel his party's warrior with sound. A glowing fungus that gathered together along a cavern wall and formed a giant spider that sprayed spores instead of webs. And that was only naming a few.

Still, he found the sight of this bald wizard disquieting.

"On behalf of my lady, I greet your grace," the bald wizard said in a voice so oily it could have kept every wheel of those carriages and carts greased across a thousand miles of dry salt flats.

"I am Quintabis," he continued, "chief adviser to her highness, Princess Sorcha Diadiniu of Kefthal. Will your grace be so kind as to join my lady in her carriage, for a word?"

"In her *carriage*," Beornric growled to Aefric. "Don't do this."

"I wouldn't refuse to meet a princess of Rethneryl this way," Aefric said softly.

"Rethneryl is our ally."

"I wouldn't refuse to meet a princess from Hatay or Shachan this way either."

"Is there a problem, your grace?' Quintabis asked.

"No problem," Aefric said, dismounting and drawing the Brightstaff from its sling.

Quintabis raised a hand in what almost looked like a halting gesture, except that it lacked commitment.

"Please, your grace," Quintabis said, bowing slightly in his saddle. "We present no threat. Surely, there is no need for your grace to carry with him ... such a weapon ... for nothing more than an exchange of a few spoken words?"

"Do you know me by reputation, Quintabis?" Aefric asked.

"Of the reputation of the current duke of Deepwater, I have heard whispers now and again."

"And of the adventurer, Aefric Brightstaff?"

"Of him," Quintabis said with another of those too-wide smiles, "I have heard a great deal though the years."

"Then certainly you have heard that where I go, the Brightstaff goes."

Quintabis bowed, even ducking his head in the process. When he came back up from his bow, he said, "And yet, never before as adventurer or duke has Aefric Brightstaff taken audience with a member of the royal house of Kefthal."

"I have carried the Brightstaff into the presence of kings and queens alike. To yield it here could be construed as placing your princess above them all. Including my own king."

"Or, perhaps," Quintabis said — though how he spoke clearly through that smile, Aefric couldn't guess — "it could be taken as a gesture of diplomatic goodwill, and a sign that your grace's intentions towards us are as peaceful as our own intentions towards your grace."

There were many things Aefric considered pointing out then. Kefthal's reputation. The whiff of necromancy in the air. The fact that he would be beyond the reach of his knights and immediate help, inside that carriage.

Instead, Aefric said simply, "The Brightstaff goes everywhere with me. If it is not allowed in that carriage, neither am I. Please tell your princess I shall be happy to meet with her another time."

He started to turn away. The watching crowd sizzled with sudden, hushed conversation.

"Wait!" Quintabis called. "Please! Your grace!"

Aefric turned back.

"Her highness informs me that your terms are acceptable."

"Very well, then," Aefric said, stepping forward.

Quintabis once more raised his hand in that weakly halting gesture.

"Forgive me, your grace. This is a small thing, beside the Brightstaff, and yet, I cannot help but note the wand your grace carries at his belt. Unless I am very much mistaken, it is the wand Garram?"

"It is," Aefric said, surprised and more than a little impressed that Quintabis could name that wand, even while it sat in a sheath at Aefric's belt.

Of course, after Frozen Ridge, word would have gotten around that he wielded the wand Garram. So Quintabis might only have been making a reasonable assumption.

"Your grace's signature tool of the Art is one matter," Quintabis said. "And her highness has proven most understanding in permitting your grace to carry it into her presence. However, I must ... raise objection to your grace carrying a secondary weapon, especially one of ... such power and repute."

Beornric started to say something, but Aefric shook his head. He drew Garram from its sheath and floated it through the air back to Beornric, for safe keeping.

Aefric noted, though, the hungry way Quintabis watched the wand as it moved.

Once this was done, Quintabis gave Aefric an exaggerated bow, and swept his arm out, inviting Aefric to enter the carriage. Aefric noticed that the man's fingernails looked long, and sharp.

Aefric walked across the cobbles. Mouth dry, and heart pounding with concern that he was making a grave mistake.

NONE OF THOSE KNIGHTS IN ENAMELED BLACK PLATE ARMOR TURNED AS Aefric walked past them. In fact, they remained impressively still. The only signs of life came from their mounts, which Aefric could see breathing and looking about. Snorting every so often.

That at least suggested that those knights were alive. Living horses generally didn't do well around the undead.

Also, Aefric understood now why he'd had trouble spotting the heraldry of their banners — they weren't carrying any. No pennants. No banners. No flying colors of any kind.

Quintabis continued giving Aefric that too-wide smile. And Aefric was close enough now to see that the bald wizard's eyes were the color of raw venison.

Tension knotted Aefric's shoulders, and roiled in his empty belly. He had to work his jaw a little, to loosen it. He felt surrounded by enemies. Turning about and flying to the keep sounded like the sanest course of action.

For the sake of all the gods, these people were from Kefthal! Did he really owe them the same level of diplomatic respect he'd give the princess from some more reasonable kingdom?

But he pressed on all the same. Step by step across the cobblestones, closing the distance. And all the while, he kept spells ready at his fingertips.

Just in case.

As he neared the ebony carriage, with its gold and silver trim, he noted the device emblazoned on its door. A circle of nine white skulls, facing the viewer, on a black background.

So they weren't traveling *completely* bereft of acknowledgments of who they were...

The carriage door opened for him.

Between Aefric and the inside was a veil of darkness. Magical, of course, and it felt like part of the carriage, rather than a specific spell. Either way, he couldn't see in, and he wondered if anyone inside could see out.

A quick moment's probing, though, proved that the veil was just a veil. No hidden secondary effects.

"Your grace's safety is, of course, guaranteed," Quintabis said from behind in. "In case such words need be said aloud."

Why didn't that feel reassuring?

Well, Aefric had come this far...

He drew a deep breath, forced his forehead muscles to relax, and stepped through the veil.

Gentle light within. Magical. Displaying a carriage interior that stood a sharp contrast to what he'd seen so far.

Rich purple silks. Thickly padded bench seats. And two occupants.

The first had to be the princess herself. A woman who looked to be no older than Aefric — though he could tell she was a magic-user of some power, which meant she might be considerably older than she looked.

Either way, she presented herself well. High cheekbones, and small, pointed chin. Long black hair that rode down over one bare shoulder, bound by gold rings. Eyes that were a bright shade of purple, and smiled as Aefric took in the sight of her.

She had a long, slender throat, decorated with a velvet choker and an eye-catching cameo depicting a broadly spreading ash tree. Below that, an ornate, bejeweled gown of dark, bloodred silk, cradling a shapely body, and cut just low enough to show an impressive amount of décolletage.

She might even have been beautiful. Save for three things. Her skin was the same, eerie shade of bone white as Quintabis'. The smile in her purple eyes had a serpentine quality. And the sense of her magic carried the taint of necromancy.

The carriage's other occupant sat on her other bare shoulder. A familiar by the feel of it. A raven which watched Aefric avidly as he entered and took his seat, facing Princess Sorcha.

"I'm afraid, your highness," Aefric said, "that I don't know the customs of Kefthal. Is it expected that I bow?"

"Oh, no," she said, her pale lips smiling in a way that echoed that serpentine aspect in her eyes. "Not in your case, your grace. We of Kefthal expect deference only from those we consider our inferiors. And that list does not include your grace, whose reputation precedes him."

She said that last part while shaking her head just slightly. Rhythmically.

Her voice was soft. Gentle, almost. And Aefric didn't believe that for a moment.

"Your highness has me at a disadvantage then," Aefric said. "For I must admit that I did not know Kefthal had any princesses at all, much less one named Sorcha Diadiniu."

"At a disadvantage, yes," she said, and her smile quirked up slightly to one side. "But not one I seek to exploit."

Aefric expected her to go on from there, but she seemed content merely to stare at him.

And she never seemed to blink.

"Your highness wished a word with me?" he asked.

"A word," she said. "Yes."

"A word!" her raven said. "A word!"

"Hush, Mizirian," she said, never looking away from Aefric. "Kefthal is loved by few, but misunderstood by many. I would invite your grace for a private tour of Kefthal, that he might learn the truth for himself."

"That is … quite an invitation," Aefric said, unable to believe what he'd just heard. Invited? To tour *Kefthal*? Obviously they would only show him what they wanted him to see—

"Yes," Princess Sorcha said. "And your grace may consider that invitation to stand, even though I do not believe he would accept."

She raised a hand before Aefric could speak.

"Or, rather," she continued, "let us say that I do not believe King Colm Stronghand would allow his greatest vassal to visit Kefthal without an army opening the way."

"Your highness has something else in mind then?"

"Yes. Something else." She smiled again, and Aefric half expected her to hiss like a snake. "I wish permission to give your grace a gift."

"A gift?"

"A gift. From the princess of Kefthal to the duke of Deepwater. A gesture of … friendship and goodwill."

"What sort of gift?"

"That would spoil the surprise, your grace." Her smile widened, but not yet enough to show teeth. "But I shall swear by the Nine that this gift shall present no threat to your grace, nor to your lands or people."

"If that's true, why do you need permission?"

"Reputation," she said, and it came out almost a whisper. "An unexpected gift arriving from Kefthal might ... provoke a reaction that could endanger the gift. Thus, I come to your grace first, seeking permission."

She had a point. Aefric could just imagine the responses of Yrsa and Beornric. They'd likely set fire to the gift without opening it. Or something equally destructive.

Still. Aefric wanted her to repeat her promise that this "gift" wouldn't present a threat. But she'd sworn by the Nine, and that sounded like the kind of oath she'd be expected to keep.

So asking her to repeat it could well be offering a dire insult.

"Was I mistaken?" Princess Sorcha asked.

"No," Aefric said. "My advisers would likely see it destroyed unopened."

"Your grace's advisers, but not your grace?"

"Let's just say I would approach it with extreme caution."

"Caution!" Mizirian croaked. "Caution!"

"A worthy answer," Princess Sorcha said with a slight nod. "May I then have permission to give your grace the gift I have in mind?"

Aefric swallowed. "I am pleased to grant this permission to your highness."

"Thank you, your grace," she said. "I shall see it to your grace's hands soon. Certainly before the Autumn Harvest Festival."

That could be anytime in the next six aetts, plus a few days.

"Then in advance, I thank you," Aefric said, fighting down the urge to bow.

"And now," she said, "I and mine shall take our leave."

"You don't intend to stay for the Feast of Dereth Sehk?"

"It is too soon for such a thing," she said. "My presence ... would cause disturbance. Perhaps even trouble."

She shook her head in that slow, rhythmic way again.

"I do not wish that," she continued. "Better that I leave."

"A thoughtful choice, and one I will not forget," Aefric said. "May your journey home be smooth and swift."

"Thank you, your grace. Enjoy the Feast."

Aefric started to get up, but frowned and turned back.

"I hesitate to mention this," he said, "but feel it is my obligation, as duke."

"By all means, your grace. Speak this obligation."

"I am obligated to inform your highness that the art of necromancy is barred throughout Armyr by royal decree. And the corresponding punishment is not gentle."

Her smile stretched just a little. Still not quite enough to show teeth. "Then I shall ensure that I and mine cast no such spells, and partake in no such rites, while within Armyr's borders."

"Thank you," Aefric said, not feeling reassured in the least.

"Your grace is kind to warn us."

As Aefric left the carriage he noticed that he *could* see out through that veil.

STEPPING OUT OF PRINCESS SORCHA'S CARRIAGE AND BACK INTO THE warm afternoon sunlight was like dunking into a welcoming hot bath after an evening traveling through freezing rain.

It shouldn't have felt that way. Not to such an extreme. The sense of necromancy inside that carriage must've been even stronger than Aefric had realized.

Subtle work then, with a powerful mind behind it...

Quintabis gave Aefric a deep bow and one more too-wide smile before saying in that unctuous voice of his, "Your grace is most kind to welcome us this way. Know that Kefthal shall not forget his kindness."

Something about the way Quintabis said, "welcome..."

It dawned on Aefric then that the nearest border of his duchy was a good fifty miles away. The nearest border of Armyr, much, much farther.

And yet this company of forty knights, a wizard, and a foreign princess had reached him without any advanced notice.

A trickle of cold fear washed down Aefric's back.

How had they managed this? And just what *else* could Kefthal do?

Quintabis must've seen the realization in Aefric's eyes, because his too-wide smile stretched a little further, and he nodded his bone-white head just a little.

Adventuring instincts flared. Made Aefric want to balance the scales a bit. A show of magic, perhaps. Some little reminder to Kefthal that Aefric Brightstaff was no one to trifle with.

He bit that down. A display like that right now — or even words to the same effect — would show fear.

And he had the feeling that showing fear to Kefthal was the worst possible mistake he could make.

So Aefric forced a smile onto his face, and hoped it looked something like his normal smile. He touched the bill of his hat in a gesture that could have been construed as acknowledging what just passed between Quintabis and himself, or as a simple gesture of farewell.

"Her highness has shown great kindness and consideration this day as well," he said. And he let his tone carry two meanings as he finished, "Neither shall I forget that."

Quintabis bowed again, which — according to Princess Sorcha — meant that Quintabis considered himself Aefric's inferior. Was that a simple fact about their relative social positions? Or was it a statement about Aefric's presumed magical power?

Or could it have been an attempt to lull Aefric into a sense of complacency, where Quintabis was concerned?

No way to tell, just now.

Brightstaff in hand, Aefric made his way back toward his horse, while Princess Sorcha's procession turned about and made their way back to the granite road and from there, presumably, the Kingsroad.

Aefric's knights and soldiers stared at him with a variety of expressions. Some awed, some concerned, others, well, Aefric could not be sure, at a glance.

Sometime during his conversation with the princess, though, the crowd of common folk had dispersed. Perhaps disappointed at the lack of a show. They'd gone back to either their work — hammers, saws, and orders rang out in the background — or their revelry. Aefric could hear their music and laughter in the distance, too.

The noise was a good thing though. Allowed Aefric to speak freely before he even reached his horse.

"I find myself wondering," he said, "just how a Kefthali princess, along with her wizard and company of *forty knights*, made it this deep into my duchy without my knowing about them."

"We've been discussing that very question, your grace," Beornric said, while the Knights of the Lake all nodded. "And with permission, I'll set about getting some answers as soon as we're settled in the tower."

"You have it," Aefric said as he mounted up and slid the Brightstaff back into its sling. "I want those answers as soon as I can get them. And while you're at it, send warning to everyone nearby to watch for them. I want to know what routes they choose, if they stay ahorse or take a boat."

He snapped his fingers for emphasis. "If they turn south and ride straight into the skies, I want to know how fast they fly. Understood?"

Beornric and the other knights all clapped their hilts in acknowledgment.

"Also," Aefric continued, "no one is to engage them, unless the Kefthali give reason." He shook his head. "I don't think they will. I think they intend to leave peacefully this time. And I don't want any of my people getting jumpy and committing an act of war."

"Yes, your grace," Beornric said, and offered back the wand Garram.

"All right," Aefric said. He sheathed his wand, then reached down and soothed his horse, which had begun snorting in time to Aefric's complaints. No reason for the poor animal to fret over its rider's worries. "I think we're ready then."

Beornric cleared his throat.

"There is one more point I must raise, your grace," he said. "I don't believe I have to mention just how risky getting into that carriage was. Nor enumerate the number of things that could have gone wrong."

"You're right," Aefric said, quirking a smile he didn't really feel. "You don't."

He snapped his reins, and led the way back toward his place in the cavalcade, which was clearly ready now to enter the courtyard of Herewyn's tower keep here at Asarchai.

About time, too.

"May I ask what her highness wanted to talk about?" Beornric said, as they rode.

"Well, she offered to give me a guided tour of Kefthal."

"Over my dead body!"

All around them, the Knights of the Lake slapped their hilts in agreement.

Aefric chuckled. "But she felt that might not be well received. So although that offer stands, she also asked permission to send me a gift."

"You refused, of course," Beornric said, scowling as though he already knew differently.

"She gave her oath first that this gift would present no threat to me, nor to my lands or people."

"You'd take *her* oath?"

"She swore on the Nine," Aefric said, shrugging one shoulder. "I figured that if any oath held meaning for her, it would be that one."

"And did you ask what she considered a threat?"

"I…" Aefric frowned.

"I thought as much," Beornric said, and grimaced. "Your grace, in politics, viewpoint is everything. It is not enough to say something is not a threat, if both sides do not first agree what defines a threat."

Aefric sighed.

"Alas, I am not finished, your grace," Beornric said.

"What else did I miss?" Aefric asked, feeling chagrined now.

"Did your grace specify that the gift must be something legal to possess in Armyr?"

"That goes without saying, doesn't it?"

"Among most kingdoms, of course," Beornric said. "But we speak of a princess from Kefthal. She might consider a company of skeletal troops a perfectly reasonable gift. And since they would be under your grace's command, she would not consider them presenting a threat to your grace, his lands, or his people."

Aefric winced. "She wouldn't."

"I would remind your grace that Duchess Ashling gave you a thank-you gift of warships. Gifts of strategic value are not uncommon among nobles."

"That gift also included a castle," Aefric said, then realized what he'd just said. "But surely ... this Princess Sorcha ... wouldn't..."

"Give your grace a gift that he must come to Kefthal to claim?" Beornric nodded his head back and forth. "It strikes me as a reasonable possibility."

Thirteen hells. Every time Aefric thought he was coming to understand what it meant to be a noble, some aspect or twist surfaced that he hadn't seen coming.

"And here I thought that I had to accept, because refusing the gift would be an insult. After all, we're not at war."

"Your grace is correct," Beornric said. "As we are not at war with Kefthal, refusing *would* have insulted them. But since the offended party would have been *Kefthal*, I think it's safe to say that King Colm would have supported your decision."

"King Colm wasn't there in the carriage."

Beornric straightened as though Aefric had slapped him.

"Forgive me, your grace," he said, managing a slight bow even as they trotted their horses. "I thought only of the gift, not of the circumstances. While your grace sat within that carriage, agreeing to accept the gift was the only reasonable course of action."

"Thank you," Aefric said. "I was starting to feel a little foolish there."

"Your grace can always refuse the gift once it arrives."

"If the gift is illegal or otherwise inappropriate."

Beornric harrumphed as though he felt Aefric should refuse the gift no matter what — and perhaps he was right — but Aefric would have at least a few aetts to consider his options. Perhaps discuss them with his other advisers as well.

Certainly his historian, Elkari Ol'Nuval, might be able to find precedents one way or the other, when it came to accepting gifts from nobles who represented undesirable alliances.

They were almost back to their proper place in the cavalcade now, and Aefric pondered Princess Sorcha's gift while he, Beornric, and the Knights of the Lake resumed their places.

Up at the front, his trumpeter raised his instrument and blew the ducal fanfare. On the side streets, some of the common folk who heard the fanfare cheered, and came to watch Aefric's formal arrival.

The cavalcade began to move slowly toward the open granite gate, leading into the keep's courtyard.

"Even if she does intend to give me lands and a castle," Aefric said, "perhaps accepting wouldn't be the worst thing. I might be able to shine some light into their darkness."

"Perhaps," Beornric said flatly. "Were your grace a mere adventurer. But can an Armyrian duke afford that investment of time and resources in another kingdom?"

"No," Aefric said with a sigh. "I suppose not."

"There's another point your grace hasn't considered," Beornric said, tugging gently at his mustache.

Aefric looked at his knight-adviser. Saw the meaning in his eyes.

"No. Surely not."

"Surely so, your grace," Beornric said with a nod that seemed to pronounce doom on Aefric. "A foreign power sent a princess to meet you, and offer a gift. I trust your grace knows by now what comes next."

"But the whole idea is ridiculous."

"It's not ridiculous, your grace. It's politics. What better way for Kefthal to expand its influence in this part of Qorunn than through marriage?"

Rikas. Beautiful birds, with their bright red crests, but that wasn't what made them valuable.

No, they were smart enough to be trained, and strong enough fliers to cross even the Risen Sea. Which made them perfect for delivering messages.

And Aefric must've spent more than an hour in the rookery of Herewyn's tower keep that day, just sending rikas.

First, he sent word about his encounter with Princess Sorcha to King Colm at Armityr, as well as his own general, Ser Yrsa, currently at Ajenmoor, Ser Grey, Aefric's castellan at Behal, and Ser Garnotin, his castellan at Water's End.

Each of those four had to know that Aefric had met with a woman said to be Kefthal's princess, that he'd declined a guided tour of her country, and that she would be sending him a gift.

Oh, and all four needed to know that *she was traveling with forty knights and a wizard.*

Not to mention that Aefric had no idea who might or might not've been in that second carriage. At the time, he'd assumed that carriage carried Princess Sorcha's ladies in waiting. Or some Kefthali equivalent. But he really had no idea if that was true.

And those carts. With most such companies, those carts would have carried supplies. Meaning, largely, food. But with a Kefthali company, what kind of supplies would they carry?

Aefric did also mention that he'd warned her against any use of necromancy while within Armyr.

Oh, yes. And that Beornric considered it likely that this was the first overture towards a possible marriage proposal.

Gods above and below, Aefric hoped it was not. Hoped that Beornric was wrong this time. Even if Princess Sorcha were not of Kefthal, Aefric was not convinced she was ... wholly human. That serpentine aspect. Those unblinking eyes. That veil, shielding her from sunlight.

And living human skin simply did not come in that shade of white.

Not that he could take time just then to contemplate the possibilities of what, exactly, Princess Sorcha was.

Aefric had more rikas to send.

His peers, Duke Wylyn Stormsent of Silverlake and Duchess Ashling Fyrenn of Merrek, needed to know that he'd received an envoy from Kefthal said to be a princess. That she'd come in peace, but come in force. That she'd arrived without warning.

And most of all, that they might receive similar envoys.

Duke Wylyn was long married, but one of his daughters was a widow. And Duchess Ashling was not yet married. If Kefthal wanted a marriage alliance in Armyr, they seemed as likely targets to Aefric as he was.

While Aefric did all this, Beornric sent a second set of rikas, trying to find out how Kefthal managed to get so large — and potentially threatening — a company so deep within Deepwater without the duke receiving warning.

Once those were flying, Beornric also sent word to every one of Aefric's major vassals, as well as the mayors of his towns and cities along rivers and the Kingsroad, the captain of his fort in Kerrik Forest, the mayor of his port city of Ajenmoor, and finally to the castellan at his majesty's closest watchtower, Towerkeep.

In Aefric's name, he ordered every one of them to keep an eye out for Princess Sorcha and her company. To watch her company should it draw near, but *not* to start trouble unless given cause.

Well, Aefric could only *recommend* this course of action to Towerkeep. The castellan there answered directly to his majesty, not to the Duke of Deepwater.

By the time all that was finished, Aefric only just had time before dinner to clean up a bit in the rooms provided for him on the top floor of the tower.

His rooms were simple, as he expected from a vassal's secondary keep. A sitting room, a bedroom, a bath, and a closet. None of them as large as he was used to, of course. But the furnishings were elegant and comfortable, and the windows along the curved outer wall large and paned with glass, with lovely views of the river, the Teryrnon Grand Theater, and the campgrounds beyond.

There was no plastering or floorboards anywhere in the keep. At least, not that Aefric had seen so far. But then, the granite was so smooth and seamless, none was really needed. There were, though, sweet-smelling rugs woven from pale green rushes.

The tapestries on the walls of Aefric's rooms depicted the growing town of Asarchai, busy river traffic, and the construction of the Teryrnon Grand Theater.

But the afternoon was growing late, and Aefric didn't have time to linger over a view or a tapestry.

In fact, he didn't have time to linger over a bath, either. Even though he could sense Burrew's magic woven through the large, copper tub, tying it into warming enchantments throughout the whole of the keep.

Such a bath would get hot quickly, and probably stay hot as long as desired. Quite a luxury, after a sweaty day on horseback.

Later for that, though.

No, feeling the need to handle his ablutions quickly, Aefric cheated. He used a little cleanliness spell he'd developed back in the early days of his first apprenticeship, in service to Karbin.

No matter how filthy Aefric's duties might have left him, Karbin would not abide a dirty apprentice. So Aefric was forced to either spend half his waking hours washing, or figure out a magical shortcut.

That was a long time ago.

Now, he needed hardly the span of three breaths to pass his hands through the air above his naked body, channeling magic that left every inch of him clean and fresh when he was finished.

Even his long, sandy blonde hair looked freshly brushed.

Tempted as he was to do the same for his clothes, he knew better. If he started using magic to do the job a servant did, he would reduce the need for servants. And thus, the number of jobs available to his people.

So he left his dusty riding clothes for the servants to launder, and wandered naked into his closet to consider his dinner wardrobe options.

Fortunately, while Aefric had been writing messages, servants had unpacked the clothing from his luggage, leaving the rest intact.

He settled on dark blue hose under a quilted, black silk tunic embroidered with silver. A soft, dark brown leather for his belt and his low shoes, with their turned-down collar.

His silver-edged noble's knife, the wand Garram, his belt pouch and the Brightstaff rounded out his outfit. Though he did also wear a ring given to him by Queen Eppida: woven from sixteen different shades of gold, it was anchored by a large emerald.

He wore very little ornamentation for a duke, he knew, but during his adventuring days he'd never gotten into the habit of wearing jewelry that didn't serve a magical purpose.

Were he back at Water's End, he would likely have let his valets hector him into wearing more. But here in Norra, he wouldn't bother for anything short of a formal event.

Dinner tonight, he'd been told, would not be formal. He could get away with just the ring.

A quick final survey in the full-length mirror in the bedroom, and he was off to see about dinner.

Outside Aefric's rooms, he was met not by four soldiers of his personal guard — as he'd expected — but by two Knights of the Lake.

The first was Ser Leppina, with her tanned skin, her strong build, and her single braid of dark brown hair that reached nearly to her hips. Aefric had been told she only cut her hair when she was defeated in single combat.

The other knight was sea-toughened Ser Micham, with his brown hair and beard both trimmed to the latest fashions, even though this kept the half-ear he'd lost to a borog's spear plain for all to see.

They were accompanied by a young page in pale blue livery who seemed to be jittering with excitement.

"Your grace!" he said, bowing so low Aefric half-expected the lad to take a knee. "I have the honor of escorting your grace to dinner."

He straightened up. Pointed the way down the hall away from the stairs Aefric had come up.

"If your grace would be so kind as to follow me this way."

"A moment," Aefric said, then, quieter, to his knights, he said, "So much for Beornric giving my Knights of the Lake a break from guard duty for the Feast, eh?"

"We requested resumption of the duty, your grace," Leppina said, "one and all."

"If Kefthal thinks to threaten our duke," Micham said, "we'll have something to say about it."

"You expect to see them again then?" Aefric asked.

"Distraction is an old tool in warfare," Leppina said. "Draw your opponent's attention to the east, then strike from the west."

"Let's hope it doesn't come to that," Aefric said, then turned to the page. "All right. Lead on."

"Yes, your grace," the page said, and his voice cracked on the words. Poor lad. He was of that age when his voice likely broke often, and a great deal of growth would follow. "This way, your grace."

Aefric repressed a smile at the lad's enthusiasm, but it wasn't easy. The page led them down the smooth hallway, warmly lit as it was by pillar candles along the walls, surrounded by curves of polished bronze. The lit candles smelled of beeswax.

The page led Aefric up a flight of stairs to the roof of the tower.

In the west, the sun was beginning to set above the sharp cliffs that separated Norra from Felspark. The air was warm, and pregnant with anticipation for the feast to come.

And the scents of dinner were savory. Aefric couldn't tell exactly what he was smelling, but there were pungent spices, and his mouth watered and stomach rumbled in anticipation.

The tower was as wide at the top as it was at the bottom. At least a hundred feet across. Wide enough that the four catapults — currently at the cardinal corners, but on wheels in case they needed to be moved — looked almost like decoration, rather than dominating the scene.

Aefric noted chainmail-clad soldiers manning those catapults as well as patrolling the crenellated edges. Likely also a response to the sudden appearance of Kefthal.

In the center of the tower's top, though, an island of calm. A raised platform, perhaps dozen strides wide, where dinner was to be held.

Along the edges of the platform, servants waited at stations where each course either stood ready or was being prepared.

In the center, a small, round table, under a pale blue cloth. Four chairs, three of whose occupants stood waiting beside those chairs.

Chief among these, of course, was the baroness herself. Herewyn had brushed out her shimmering red hair, and let it fall, fanning out behind her and standing a sharp contrast to her pale green, velvet gown. A sapphire dangled at the end of a gold chain around her neck, teasing along her low neckline, and a simple gold diadem crowned her.

Herewyn looked regal, standing there with the sun at her back, and the smile she gave Aefric was both proud and pleased.

To Herewyn's left stood Sighild. She, too, had brushed out her hair. But rather than having it fan out behind her, she draped some of it forward over her bare shoulders, where it combined with the pale peach color of her silk corset and skirts — so close to her own skin tone — to call to mind the first time Aefric had seen her unclothed.

She'd been standing near the door to his bedroom at Water's End. The servants had just left the room. Aefric himself had been clad in only a dressing gown, following a bath, when she'd walked into the room, undid the two ties on her simple gown, and let her outfit drop to pool on the floorboards at her feet.

And standing there on the dais, in the late afternoon sunlight, Sighild gave Aefric a smile that let him know her dress and hair had been arranged exactly to call that memory to his mind.

To Herewyn's right stood a man Aefric hadn't met. Perhaps a handful of years older than the baroness, he had the pale skin of a noble, with a jet black mustache and beard combination that Keifer would have called a Van Dyke. His hair was curly, and hung just shy of his collar.

And the man wore a wide collar, the yellow-white shade of aged parchment, like the shirt that bloused out under his black velvet doublet. His hose were matching black, and though the women had come unarmed to the dinner table, he wore a longsword at his hip. He wore a single gold ring, with a large diamond, on the index finger of his right hand.

Aefric mounted the stairs to the dais. He acknowledged the bows of the other three diners with a nod, and sat, allowing them to sit as well.

They didn't.

Instead, Herewyn rounded the table and stood beside Aefric, who was caught between standing again and turning his chair to face her.

He turned his chair, figuring that a duke shouldn't stand immediately after being seated. Not for anything less than royalty.

Herewyn seemed to expect this. Or at least, she gave no sign that she expected Aefric to do anything else.

"Your grace," she said, "I know I said that this dinner would be informal. And I devoutly hope your grace will allow it to be. But there is one detail of business that tradition requires of me before informality is an option."

Suspecting he knew what this business was, Aefric nodded.

Herewyn looked deeply into Aefric's eyes, and knelt smoothly at his feet. She offered her hand, as vassal to liege, and he kissed it, showing he was pleased with her. She pressed her forehead briefly to his knuckles, to emphasize her loyalty, before releasing his hand.

"My liege," she said warmly, "this keep is yours, as indeed is all of Asarchai and Norra beyond."

Yes. The same little ritual she'd performed at Norrtarr the night before. Technically, all of his vassals were to do something like this when he stayed at their keeps, but Herewyn always seemed to get a little more out of it.

"Thank you, my baroness, my faithful and trusted vassal," Aefric said. "And know that all of Deepwater values the work you do here."

Aefric held out his hand to her. Herewyn didn't need it, to rise. He knew that. But offering his hand felt polite, and he liked the small smile she gave him as she took it.

He felt no pull on his grip at all as she rose smoothly to her feet. She took off the diadem, and without looking offered it to a servant who stepped up to take it.

She shook out her hair, not that it needed it.

She took her seat then, and Sighild and the nobleman sat down with her.

"Your grace," Herewyn said, still smiling, "may I present my cousin, Ler Gwalter Ol'Norette."

"Your grace," Gwalter said, bowing in his seat. "I have heard a good deal about Deepwater's new duke, and all of it good."

"Then I suspect at least some of it has been lies," Aefric said with a smile. "But please, if this is to be an informal dinner, let us dispense with titles and courtesies for the evening."

"Thank you, Aefric," Herewyn said, while Gwalter looked at Aefric as though reassessing him.

Servants brought the palate wine then. A small glass — hardly more than a swallow — of gentle white wine intended to symbolically wash away the cares of the day while preparing the taste buds for dinner.

The palate wine was drunk in contemplative silence — the Norra way — and then the first course of the meal. A salad of crisp mixed greens and seasoned root vegetables, topped with a just a hint of oil, to bring out all the natural flavors.

To drink with the salad, a type of wine called sharabi. Sharabi could come in a variety of shades as well as flavors, and this sharabi was pale green, light, and had an undertaste that made Aefric think of walnuts.

This was the beginning of a marvelous dinner. A main course of seasoned river trout that was thick as a steak, but so light and buttery that it seemed to melt in Aefric's mouth. It was served with a mix of roasted corn and tara, and honeyed oat bread so fresh its smell alone seemed to relax a part of Aefric that had been tense since he first heard that strange fanfare only a few hours prior.

And the conversation was as good as the meal.

Aefric told some of the lighter stories from his adventuring days. Such as the one about Denevon, the skald he knew who'd stopped two men from dueling to the death over water rights by seducing them both. Then the next morning, convincing them to get married instead of dueling. Happy endings all around.

Sighild told stories about amusing misunderstandings and errant love letters among the minor nobles at the royal court in Armityr.

Herewyn told stories of strange things said to have happened in Kerrik Forest. Of trees that sang when the light hit them just so, and rabbits who could grant wishes, when saved from a snare.

Best of these, in Aefric's mind, was the farmer whose farm had failed, sending him far east and into the woods to trap dinner for his table.

Well, the farmer's best efforts had yielded only the one rabbit. Hardly enough for himself, let alone his family. But he took out his knife and prepared to make do when the rabbit had shocked him by speaking the common tongue.

"Wait!" the rabbit cried, and told the tale of his magic, and how he could grant the farmer a single wish, if only the farmer would release him.

Well, the farmer had never heard of a talking rabbit, so he agreed. And the wish he spoke was this: "Let the ground yield its riches for me once more, beyond any it ever gave up for even my forefathers."

The rabbit promised that it would be so, and the farmer released him.

The farmer went home to dig, and test the land. But when he dug, he struck pure, strong marble.

The farmer would become a rich man, and Norra would become famous for its twin quarries: granite and marble.

Gwalter contributed little to the conversation that night. He seemed overwhelmed to be at an informal dinner with his duke, and opted to listen instead of speaking.

But at least the man was an appreciative audience. He listened attentively, laughed when appropriate, and seemed to hang on every story. Even the ones he'd doubtless heard before.

Overall, just the kind of dinner Aefric needed after a trying afternoon.

After a full and satisfying dinner — both socially and gustatorily — Aefric retired to his chambers for the evening, where two soldiers of Aefric's personal guard already stood watch.

"All clear," one of them — Tora, if Aefric recalled correctly — said to the knights.

With his knights on a higher level of alert now, Leppina checked his rooms while Micham remained with Aefric and the two soldiers in the hall, before returning to say that all was well.

Aefric, who felt he'd shown great patience in tolerating the delay, said, "Was that necessary?"

"It was, your grace," Leppina said with a single nod. "Ser Beornric said we were to take no chances. That we could not be sure of Kefthal's goals or capabilities."

"Or, for that matter," Micham said, "that Motte will..." He turned to Leppina. "How did Beornric phrase it?"

"Ah, 'that Motte will behave himself,' I believe."

"Yes," Micham said. "That was it. While our captain did not wish to level any accusations against your grace's ... most recalcitrant vassal, neither did he feel we should assume that said vassal would behave ... appropriately."

"I believe," Leppina said, "he still harbors a grudge against Count Ferrin for trying to goad your grace into battle before even officially taking up your grace's ducal seat at Water's End."

Aefric looked from one knight to the other and back.

"You two want to stand guard inside the sitting room, don't you." He didn't make it a question.

Leppina and Micham glanced at each other. Micham gave her a

slight nod.

"That might be preferable, your grace," Leppina said. "Under the circumstances."

"And we have Tora and Ander, here, to handle door duty," Micham added.

"Fine," Aefric said. "Just don't kill anyone without permission."

"Of course, your grace," Leppina said lightly.

"Wouldn't dream of it, your grace," Micham said, in the same tone.

The knights followed Aefric inside.

The chamber servants were already finished and gone, though they'd left Aefric a full, steaming tub of water in the bath.

Oh, but that was a good idea. A good soak sounded like just the way to end his day, and even from the bedroom, he could smell fragrant wisteria, added to the bathwater.

Without delay, Aefric stripped down, left the Brightstaff standing beside his bed, and strode into his bath chamber.

Fluffy white towels had been stacked on a shelf beside the steaming copper tub. Beside them, a thick, heavy bar of soap that looked to have herbs mixed inside it. On a peg hung a sheer white linen dressing gown, and a heavier, navy blue robe.

Sinking down into that hot, welcoming tub was pure delight. And yet, Aefric had to laugh at himself.

He'd been getting spoiled by life at Water's End.

This copper tub was not only long enough that Aefric could lie down in it completely, should he choose to, but it was wide enough that he didn't feel hemmed in on the sides.

The kind of tub he'd yearned for on cold, rainy nights when he'd been slogging through mud during his adventuring days, or during the wars.

And yet, now this tub felt small to him. Quaint, beside the gigantic marble tub he had at Water's End. Where he also had a commanding view of Lake Deepwater, and beyond.

Whereas here, in this tub, he had only a series of gentle landscape paintings for his view.

He enjoyed his bath all the same, of course. Scrubbing tired muscles in water just this side of too-hot was always a pleasure. As was just sitting, and soaking, and relaxing away some of the cares of his day.

The enchantments Burrew had lain on the tub did their work well. Aefric soaked in that tub for quite some time, and yet the heat never diminished.

Aefric's fingers were beginning to prune when he decided to do one last thing before getting out.

He cast a spell that would carry his words directly to his intended listener, and allow her to respond in kind.

On the one hand, a marvelously efficient form of communication. But its limitations kept him from using it often.

First, he could never be sure what the recipient would be doing when contact was made. Potentially dangerous, if distraction came at the wrong time. Or at the very least, inconvenient.

Second, the message would not be repeated. So if it came in and the listener needed a moment before she could pay attention, critical words might be lost.

Third, no record of the message would exist. So the spell couldn't be used for anything official.

And those were only the top three of the limitations inherent to the magic.

But it had its time and its place. And right now, Aefric needed to reach out to Byrhta. To let her know he'd heard about her father, and that he was thinking of her.

Yes, he'd sent a rika. But the rika would need time to reach Castle Vabarett. Perhaps a full day. Byrhta deserved more consideration than that.

So he cast the fifty-word version of this spell, and spoke to her from the tub.

"My dear Byrhta. I only just heard tell of your father's failing health. Please convey him my best wishes. Know that I miss you sorely, and lament that you cannot join me at the Feast of Dereth Sehk. I yearn to see you soon. You may reply with fifty words."

Whatever Byrhta was doing when Aefric's words reached her, it could not have been important. Her reply came right away.

"Oh, my sweetest Aefric, always do I long to hear your voice. But I've had no recent news of Father's health, and am not in Goldenfall. I wondered that neither Vercy nor I were invited to the Feast. Now I understand. Once more, beloved, others conspire to keep us apart."

Unfair, that so beautiful a voice should be bringing Aefric such infuriating news.

Aefric was tempted to simply gather his people and leave. Perhaps ride for Riverbreak instead, and visit both Byrhta and Vercy.

No. That was thinking like an adventurer, not a duke. Aefric had already come all this way from Water's End. He owed it to the *people* of Norra to stay, and attend the celebration of their ancestors' victory over the forces of that evil derekek emperor.

But their baroness could still be made to answer for this.

Aefric was so angry that the Brightstaff flew in from the bedroom to stand ready beside him while he toweled himself dry and donned the navy blue robe that had been left for him.

The Brightstaff followed at his heels as he strode purposefully into the sitting room of his chambers, where Leppina and Micham stood guard, inside the door to the hallway.

"Send for the baroness," Aefric said. "I want her at once. And when she comes, you two wait in the hall until I tell you otherwise. What I have to say to her isn't for others' ears."

"Your grace," Leppina began, hesitantly.

"We are on the fourth floor of a tower, guarded by soldiers above and below," Aefric said impatiently. "Any threat that reaches me here will be magical, not military, and I *should* be able to handle it."

Leppina and Micham looked at each other, uncertain.

Aefric blew out a harsh breath.

"I am quite fond of all my Knights of the Lake," he said, his tone low and dangerous. "And so I afford you all more leeway than perhaps I ought. But just in case I have not made myself clear. *This is not a request.*"

"Yes, your grace," both Micham and Leppina said at once, and bowed, before leaving the room to carry out his orders.

Aefric paced as he waited.

Aefric was not kept waiting long. He'd only paced perhaps a dozen circuits of the smallish, candlelit sitting room when there was a soft knock at the hallway door.

"Yes," Aefric said.

Leppina opened the door and leaned in. "Your grace, Baroness Herewyn arrives in response to your summons."

"Send her in," Aefric said.

Herewyn came in smiling. Her tresses down and flowing freely past her shoulders. She was clad in what looked like gauzy white linen under a thick, gray robe that she made little effort to hold closed, as she entered.

"Your grace," she said warmly, with a small bow. "I am both pleased and honored to be…"

Her words faltered, and her expression clouded as she took Aefric's posture, and the anger in his eyes.

"Have I somehow given offense, your grace?" she asked carefully. "For I begin to suspect I have not been summoned for the noble privilege."

Aefric pointed to an armchair at one end of the coffee table, under the large, curved window. Out beyond was the starry night sky, and an excellent view of the countless campfires and cookfires in the campgrounds, as well as the lights of a town beginning its celebration a little early.

Aefric took the seat facing her. The other armchair, on the other side of the table, leaving empty the small couch that faced the window.

The Brightstaff stood beside him. Waiting.

"Your grace," Herewyn said softly, "I am frightened. Please tell me how I have given offense so that I may make restitution and, gods willing, restore myself to your good graces."

"Byrhta Ol'Caran is not in Goldenfall."

"I'm ... afraid I don't understand."

To her credit, she did look puzzled. But then, Aefric was coming to understand that nobles had to be skilled and accomplished liars.

"Your lordship" — Herewyn's eyes widened to hear Aefric speak so formally — "knows that I am a magic-user. Surely she must know that I have means of communication a great deal faster and more reliable than rikas and messengers. When I wish to employ them."

"I know that your grace's powers are many," Herewyn said, "but I do not pretend to know their full scope, nor their limits. If your grace tells me he has this power, I am confident that he has it."

"I possess a spell," Aefric said then, "that allows for a brief exchange of words with someone I know well. I cast that spell tonight that I might tell Byrhta of my good wishes for her father's health, offer my assistance, if needed, and make clear my desire to see her again soon."

"Your grace is most kind," Herewyn said carefully.

"Imagine my surprise when her response told me that she was not in Goldenfall, but in Riverbreak. That she had had no recent news of her father's health. And that, though she serves as Baroness Regent of Riverbreak, she received no invitation to the Feast of Dereth Sehk this year."

"I don't understand," Herewyn said, frowning.

"I imagine that your lordship is a great deal smarter than that," Aefric said.

Herewyn's green eyes rounded wide. She dropped to her knees on the rug of woven rushes.

"Your grace," she said, imploring, "I swear upon my title, upon my family name, and upon the oaths that bind us that this is the first I am hearing of any of this. I swear also that I gave no order to exclude Riverbreak from the Feast invitations this year, and was both surprised and disappointed to learn that Riverbreak would not attend."

Again, she seemed frustratingly sincere. But how much of that could Aefric trust?

Perhaps a sideways question could tip the truth, one way or another?

"Why disappointed?" he asked.

"I was never overfond of her father, Karmody, when he was Riverbreak's baron," Herewyn said. "But I always thought that Vercy showed promise. I looked forward to seeing how she was flourishing without the ... suppressive influence of her father."

"So you gave no direct orders to exclude her or Byrhta."

"Your grace," Herewyn said, still kneeling before him, "I gave no direct or indirect orders for any such thing."

She shook her head hard enough to make her hair fly.

"Your grace," she said, "I swear I am playing no word games to hide guilt. I am as I have been, your faithful vassal. What I told your grace about the reasons for the absence of Byrhta Ol'Caran are *exactly* those I was told myself."

"So you're saying someone did this for you."

Understanding seemed to begin with the unfurrowing of Herewyn's brow, and spread to her eyes, the set of her jaw, even her posture as she knelt before her duke.

She sighed. "I do not believe this was done for *me*, your grace."

"Meaning?" Aefric said, but he gestured for her to rise. "And please, be seated as you explain."

"My thanks, your grace," she said, her voice still careful as she rose smoothly and returned to sit on her chair with perfect posture.

"Your grace," she said through another sigh, "my cousin Sighild has been a welcome guest in Norra since my mother ruled these lands. Many of the servants in my castles knew her as a bright and beautiful child. Kind, eager, and smiling at everyone."

Aefric had no trouble believing Sighild was that kind of child. Which meant...

"She is much beloved here," Herewyn said. "And I believe word has spread that she has recently become ... a close friend to your grace."

"I see," Aefric said. "So if she asked them to lose that invitation, it would never be sent, and they would be happy to present a cover story for her."

"Your grace," Herewyn said, raising her hands haltingly. "I do not mean to imply that Sighild is behind this. I suspect that ... certain others may have taken actions on her behalf. Actions I don't believe she would approve of."

"What makes you say so?" Aefric said. "She wouldn't be the first to take such actions out of fear of Byrhta's beauty."

Aefric almost went on to tell how Zoleen Fyrenn had applied pressure to Iers in Riverbreak to take steps that kept Byrhta there, rather than visiting Aefric at Water's End while their majesties visited. And, of course, while Zoleen was there, trying to win Aefric's love.

But that was a matter between himself and Zoleen.

Herewyn's reaction to the idea, though, was the last thing Aefric expected.

She laughed in what seemed like open, honest surprise.

"Oh, your grace," Herewyn said, smiling for the first time in a while now. "To see Byrhta Ol'Caran is to look upon legendary beauty made flesh. None would deny it. But to say that Sighild would shy away from competition of *any* sort. Well. The first day of the Feast of Dereth Sehk is devoted to games. Watch my cousin tomorrow, and then tell me your grace believes Sighild would refuse to face *any* challenger head-on."

Something in the way Herewyn said that managed to reach through Aefric's anger. Although, to be fair, he'd come closer and closer to believing Herewyn, the more she spoke.

Still…

"Competition in games is not the same as competition in love," Aefric said.

"In my family, they are one and the same, your grace," Herewyn said, more serious now. "My dear Garriston, may the gods hold him close, dueled no fewer than ten men while courting me. And not all of those duels involved combat."

There were a number of points in there for Aefric to absorb. He'd heard that Herewyn had been widowed, but he'd never known anything about her husband. More important right then, though, was this.

"To marry into your family, suitors duel each other?"

"It's not so simple as that, your grace," Herewyn said with a smile. "In the early stages of courting, though, suitors may indeed contest with one another to establish ... an order to things."

Aefric chuckled. "So, you could have been looking at five men, all hoping to become Norra's new baronet, and rather than giving them all equal opportunity, you would have let them fight for a place in line?"

"Thus has it been done in Norra since before the formation of Armyr. And mine is not the only family that follows this tradition."

"So when you say that Sighild wouldn't shy away from competition..."

"Oh, yes," Herewyn said, smiling wider now. "She would have waited for Byrhta to arrive, then asked your permission to duel her for priority."

"Really?"

"She would have allowed Byrhta to choose weapons, of course," Herewyn said. "The contest must be fair, to be meaningful." Her smile faded as she met Aefric's eyes again. "Which is why I know she had no knowledge of this, and gave no consent to it. Doubtless she was looking forward to impressing you, by overcoming Byrhta in a contest of Byrhta's own choosing."

"I find myself inclined to believe you," Aefric admitted.

"Your grace's faith is of paramount importance to me," Herewyn said. "As such, allow me to offer this freely. I am given to understand that your grace can command a flying chariot, yes?"

In fact, Aefric had a magic crystal that would allow him to summon a *magari*, a flying, fiery chariot, pulled by a pair of phantasmal horses known as *magaunts*.

He nodded.

"Then your grace should know that his majesty's justiciar is currently in residence at Towerkeep. A good two-day ride by horse, but likely only hours by flying chariot."

Herewyn looked deeply into Aefric's eyes.

"I swear here and now that, if your grace desires, I shall not move from this spot until he returns with the justiciar. Further, that I shall willingly submit myself to questioning on this topic under the three-edged sword of Taesark."

Taesark, the god of justice. It was said that his holy justiciars could ferret out truth even from one who has heard only lies.

For any noble to make such an offer was extreme.

"That will not be necessary," Aefric said.

Herewyn must've been holding her breath, because she exhaled pure relief.

Aefric couldn't blame her. He'd given testimony to a justiciar before, and even though he hadn't been the one under suspicion, the sensations were still not ones he would seek again.

"I trust, however," he said, "that I can count on your finding those responsible?"

"I swear it, your grace," Herewyn said. "I shall see to it that those responsible are found and punished appropriately."

"Thank you," Aefric said.

"Nothing more than my duty, your grace, and unworthy of thanks."

Aefric caught her then, glancing down from his eyes to where his robe had gaped open a bit, over his chest, showing the edges of two of his scars.

Caught looking, she held her gaze where it was and said, "It occurs to me that your grace has been caused a great deal of agitation by those in my service."

"You're not wrong," Aefric said. One of Keifer's old phrases, coming out by reflex, but it must've amused Herewyn, because she gave him a small smile.

"I would be a poor hostess, to send your grace to his bed, in such a state of agitation."

Aefric was still deciding what to say in response when she stood.

Even her bare feet were smooth, and well-shaped.

"Alas, Octave isn't here to offer your grace *leaba*, as she is so fond of doing," Herewyn said, holding her robe closed as she slowly stepped forward, still talking. "I suppose I could rouse my serving girls. I'm sure many would be most eager to take Octave's place."

Aefric found himself more and more aware of just how beautiful and graceful Herewyn was. She was like the woman Sighild would grow into in ten years. And Sighild was already impressive…

"But why should I rouse them? When I would be more than happy to attend your grace's needs tonight myself. And I've already drunk my nysta tea."

She threw off her robe.

In the candlelight, her white linen dressing gown was so sheer it both displayed her curves in detail, and yet concealed them in maddening shadows.

"If such a notion pleases your grace," she said, fire in both her eyes and voice.

"It pleases me a great deal," Aefric said with a growl.

AEFRIC WAS TEMPTED TO JUST RIP THAT THIN LINEN RIGHT OFF OF Herewyn's body. To pick her up over one shoulder and carry her to bed and find out, firsthand, just how different from Sighild she really was.

But before he could even stand up from the armchair, Herewyn held out one hand in invitation. In the heat in her green eyes, he could see a plan, and found he was quite curious about what that plan was.

He took her hand but, as she had done earlier, stood without aid.

Herewyn led him into the bedroom.

The bed was not nearly so large as what he was used to at Water's End. But then, at Water's End, the bed Aefric inherited would have been big enough to share with several companions without it feeling crowded.

Still. This bed, here in the tower at Asarchai, was certainly big enough, and comfortable enough, to meet his needs for the next few days.

Candles were lit in sconces around the room, giving the chamber both a soft, warm glow, and a faint smell of beeswax.

At the foot of the bed, Herewyn reclaimed her hand. Took hold of the ties of his robe, instead.

"May I, your grace?" she asked.

"You may," Aefric said. "But I think we can forgo courtesies tonight."

"With permission, your grace, I'd rather not," she said. "Not tonight, at least."

"Are you certain?" Aefric asked. "I wouldn't want to think you were treating this as some sort of obligation to your liege lord."

"Oh, no, your grace," she said quickly, making sure to look Aefric in the eye as she said it. "Nothing like that. In fact, when I thought your grace was summoning me here for the noble privilege, I was pleased beyond words. To share the bliss moment with your grace…"

She sighed as she looked him over. "A pleasure most enticing."

"Then why?"

"It is … difficult to explain," she said. "In my youth, Deepwater was ruled by Duchess Arinda. And my nearest neighbor not of Deepwater has always been Duchess Ashling, of Merrek."

She tilted her head to one side, smiling a little quizzically.

"I have known only duchesses, until Deepwater was given to your grace. I find … serving under a duke…" — she toyed with the ties of Aefric's robe, while looking at what she could see of the flesh beneath — "pleasing, in unexpected ways."

"Do you mind if I continue to call you Herewyn?"

"Oh, your grace, I prefer hearing my name to my title, when it comes from your lips."

"Very well, then. I believe, Herewyn, I just gave you permission to untie my robe and remove it."

"Yes, your grace," she said, and untied the belt with unhurried movements. She drew a long, deep breath and, eyes riveted on his body, slowly opened his robe.

"I have only ... known wizards ... to be soft. Skinny or fat," she said, slowly shaking her head as she looked Aefric from ankle to collarbone and back. "Never have I dreamed a wizard could possess such lean, strong muscles."

Aefric chuckled softly. How often had he heard words like those?

Of course, technically, he was a dweomerblood, not a wizard, but there was little point in correcting her. As Aefric was the first, few even knew what a dweomerblood was.

"Only wizards living in towers and keeps can afford to grow soft," he said. "Wizards who go adventuring have their bodies hardened by the lifestyle."

"So I see," she said, running her fingers along a hard, white scar left low on his right side by a sword, years ago.

He chuckled. "And I suppose it doesn't hurt that I trained as a dweomerblade."

"I wondered," she said, stepping around behind Aefric and pulling the robe down off his shoulders, "why your grace wore a sword when first I saw him."

"Habit," Aefric said, suddenly finding himself naked, with the robe pooling at his feet. "Though I continue to train regularly with the sword, and other weapons. I have no intention of letting castle life make me soft."

Herewyn made a small sound of approval, and began running her spread hands slowly down his back.

"I don't wear a sword in public these days," he continued, "because my knights prefer that I leave the sword work to them."

"Your grace is kind to indulge them," she said, her voice a little huskier now, as her hands ran over his backside and down his thighs.

"I do hope," he said archly, "that I won't be the only one naked tonight."

He suddenly felt the heat of her whole body close behind his. The soft touch of thin fabric between them.

"Oh, no, your grace," she whispered in his ear. "But first I must see about the tension I and mine have caused."

"Relieving such tension is rarely done from behind."

Herewyn chuckled, soft and warm and tickling at his ear.

"Oh, I'll get to *that* tension soon enough, your grace," she said. "And I look forward to doing so. But first, there is the matter of the other tensions caused tonight."

With pressing hands, she encouraged Aefric to lie down on the bed, face first.

Aefric did so, but as he settled in, he said, "This is not the most comfortable position in my current state."

"More comfortable, I suspect, than tight leather riding pants," Herewyn said, moving onto the bed beside him. "And yet, I did not hear your grace complain about the teasing my cousin gave him on today's lunch break."

Aefric smiled at the memory. They'd been stopped under a copse of larches, and Aefric hadn't thought anyone had seen the private moment he'd shared with Sighild before they'd mounted up to ride again.

"Some discomforts are more pleasant than others," he said.

"Then let this discomfort become pleasant in your grace's thoughts," she said, "for I shall see to it that discomfort now leads to bliss later."

"Very well," Aefric said with a sigh.

"Marvelous. Thank you, your grace," she said, and then she swung one knee over Aefric to sit on his butt, pressing him down further into the mattress there.

Now, ordinarily, Aefric very much enjoyed having a woman sit on him this way. Of course, ordinarily he'd've been flipped over, and facing her.

But right now? With that part of him pressing into the feather mattress so?

"Herewyn, what are you—"

The question died as she answered without words.

She began to knead the muscles low on his back with hands that were stronger than he expected.

He let out a long, slow groan of relief. He hadn't even realized how tense those muscles were.

"Better, your grace?"

"In some ways, very much so," he said.

She leaned down, licked his earlobe, and whispered. "I'm glad only in some ways, your grace. I wish to ease the tensions in your grace's muscles before we seek deeper pleasures, not waste an early fulfillment into nothing more interesting than my mattress."

Without waiting for a response, she sat up again and began to massage Aefric in earnest. And oh, she knew a thing or two about massage. She knew all the right muscle groups to work, and she knew how to work them well. With her fingers, palms, wrists, even her elbows.

By the time she stopped, Aefric felt far better than even he'd expected. Between Count Ferrin's arrival and attitude, that Kefthal business, and then learning that Byrhta had again been kept away from him by manipulation, he'd grown even more tense than he'd realized.

But Herewyn did an excellent job of working all of that tension out of his muscles.

Once she'd finished, she knelt beside him and trailed her fingernails lightly across his skin.

"Your grace feels more relaxed, I hope?" she asked in a teasing tone.

"Much more relaxed," he said. "In fact, I think there's only one area of tension that still requires your attention…"

"Oh?" Herewyn said, and Aefric could hear the smile in her voice. "Then your grace should roll over and let me see to this tension."

Aefric rolled over, to see her hair loose and a little wild, much like the eager smile in her eyes.

And yet, she was still wearing that nearly sheer dressing gown.

Aefric reached for her. She caught his wrists.

"If I might beg an indulgence from your grace," she said.

"Speak it," Aefric said.

"I would next relieve the … urgency from your grace's needs, that he might take as much time in exploring me as I got to spend exploring him."

"What did you have in mind?" he asked.

Herewyn smiled, and leaned in and kissed him. Oh, but it was a good kiss. Slow and lingering and inviting in ways that he could enjoy in the moment even while it made him look forward to other activities.

She came up from the kiss, and he said, softly, "That's not an answer."

"Isn't it, your grace?" she asked, kissing him next on the collarbone, and flicking her tongue over a bit of scar.

As she continued to kiss her way down his chest, it became quite clear what answer she had in mind.

Aefric found himself looking forward to that a great deal. Though she seemed in no hurry to begin…

When his turn came, Aefric tried to spend even more time pleasing Herewyn than she'd spent on him. Partially just for her, but also to help ensure that he never confused her with her younger cousin, Sighild.

It helped, initially, that Herewyn wore the scent of hyacinth, while Sighild preferred lilac. Even when his face was buried in all that shimmering red hair as he nibbled along her smooth, pale throat, one whiff was enough to ensure he didn't mistake the woman he'd begun exploring.

And once things began in earnest, all possibility of error fell quickly by the wayside.

Herewyn and Sighild may have shared a certain amount of physical resemblance, but they were nothing alike as lovers.

Sighild was always a little timid until drawn out, when she became wild and expressive. Like a fire that had to be coaxed to life, but then flared, and burned bright and roaring. And maybe a little dangerous.

Herewyn was passionate, but deliberate. Controlled. She never left any doubt about what she liked and what she didn't, but always in a way that simply encouraged more of what she enjoyed.

This was the reason he left her with several bite marks on the insides of her thighs. She seemed quite happy about each of them.

In much the same way, she seemed to study Aefric's reactions to everything she did, as though determined to know all the best ways to please him before even half the night was gone.

Aefric and Herewyn came together as lovers twice that night before pausing for rest. But at their first rest, they sat side by side, pillows propped behind them, and sipped a sweet white wine that she must've sent for at some point.

Or maybe the bottle had already been in the room, and Aefric hadn't noticed it? He certainly hadn't gone through the bedroom's contents thoroughly before dinner. And after, well, he'd been a little distracted...

"There is something I should make clear to your grace," Herewyn said, playing her toes along his shin.

"And what is that?" Aefric asked, letting his eyes track over her delightfully naked and glistening body.

"Your grace," she said softly.

"Pardon me," he said, meeting her eyes with a smile. "I was considering how the wine would go with the taste of your breasts."

"Well," Herewyn said with a smile, "I certainly encourage your grace to find out. But first..."

"I am listening," he said.

"I want to be clear about something. A great many of the noblewomen who seek out your grace's bed hold, within their hearts, some degree of hope that they might one day become your duchess."

"I assure you. I figured that out some time ago."

"I never doubted it." She leaned forward slightly. "But I wish to make clear that I, myself, do not."

"No?" Aefric asked, a little surprised. He'd been sure that, come morning, Beornric would be adding Herewyn's name to the list of women trying to marry him.

"Not as a slight against your grace in any way," she said quickly. "If anything, I find your grace almost too appealing, on a personal level."

She smiled wistfully.

Aefric gave her time to continue, if she wanted to.

"Your grace reminds me somewhat of my dearest Garriston, may the gods hold him close." She played her fingers over Aefric's chest, circling a scar left by a tarok's spear. "He too was tall, and leanly muscled. Though he had fewer scars. While he lived."

"He died in the wars, I believe," Aefric said, voice hushed out of respect.

"Two days before the Battle of Deepwater," she said. "The borog armies were on the march across Goldenfall, and Garriston led a company that gave their lives buying time for hundreds of farmers and townsfolk to flee to safety within the city walls at Vabarett."

"He died a hero," Aefric said.

"He did," Herewyn said. Her fingers withdrew. She sipped her wine, then shook her head. "But dead is dead. And the shameful truth is that I would trade all those farmers and townsfolk to have my husband back."

"I don't think anyone would blame you for feeling that way," Aefric said.

"Ah," Herewyn said, smiling through unshed tears, "but a noble isn't *supposed* to feel that way, your grace, even in private. A noble must be ready to lay down her life for her people, as we ask our people to lay down their lives for us."

"Laying down one's own life for others is easy," Aefric said. "Laying down the life of a loved one for others is another matter altogether."

Herewyn's perfect posture slumped as she stared, slack-jawed at Aefric.

"Your grace *does* understand," she said.

"I ... have known loss," Aefric said, and had to check himself from telling her about Andi, the wife he'd loved a world away. "I think sometimes that I so willingly risk myself for others because part of me hopes to be rejoined with her."

"She will be waiting, your grace," Herewyn said, softly. "Whether your grace meets her again tomorrow, or a thousand years from now, she will be waiting. As Garriston waits for me."

Herewyn reached out and stroked Aefric's face. "And on behalf of all those who remain in this world, I ask that your grace resist the urge to fly too soon to her side. Your grace is needed here."

"I have no wish to die," Aefric said, and it was his turn for a wistful smile. "Too many responsibilities."

"Just so," she said, with a half-hearted smile, that grew teasing only a moment later. "Besides, your grace, here you have the prospect of finding love again. And a great many candidates to choose from."

"But not you?"

"No, your grace," Herewyn said, not rising to Aefric's return teasing. "I love Norra, and I love being its baroness. I look forward to training my son Gariss for the day he takes over."

She shook her head. "I want neither the power nor the responsibility of being your duchess. Neither do I wish to be the secondary title holder in a relationship. If I marry again, my husband will answer to me, not the other way around."

"And you might marry again?"

"I won't rule out the possibility," Herewyn said with a slight shrug, and her posture resumed its normal perfection. "But I'm in no hurry, either. One advantage of the noble privilege, I need not be lonely while I consider my options."

She set her half-full glass on the nightstand.

"Speaking of the noble privilege," she said, lying back at an angle and giving Aefric a come-hither look. "I believe your grace said something about my skin and his wine?"

"I did indeed," Aefric said, leaning in for a kiss on her soft, welcoming lips. And as they kissed, he slowly, carefully poured the rest of his wine down into the hollow of her throat, from where it spread down across her shivering breasts and belly.

He smiled at the sight. "This may take some time."

"By all means, your grace," she answered, "be thorough."

Later, when they once more rested after satisfaction, Herewyn lay pillowing her head on Aefric's chest when she spoke.

"As your grace now knows that I have no aspirations of being his duchess," she said, idly playing with his chest hair, "he should know that I am most willing to discuss my views of his candidates, if he has a mind to hear them."

"I find myself quite curious," Aefric said, and Herewyn seemed to enjoy the way his chest rumbled when he spoke. He ran one hand down her side in a gentle caress. "Though I suspect those views will direct me to marry your cousin."

"Sighild has a great deal to offer as a candidate," Herewyn said. "But she's not where I'd begin the discussion."

"Where then?"

"Princess Maev, of course," Herewyn said, smiling. "Surely your grace must realize that all of Armyr talks of how she favors him. Of how your grace might have won her heart — were it hers to give."

"Varondam," Aefric said with a sigh.

"Varondam," Herewyn agreed, patting his hip sympathetically. "After Malimfar's treachery this past spring, Armyr needs alliance with Varondam, to surround their enemy along the coast. Those facts are indisputable."

"They are," Aefric said with another sigh.

She shook her head. "And Varondam has a prince, but not a princess. So it is Princess Maev who must ... cement this alliance through marriage. Prince Killian cannot."

"She might be able to arrange the alliance without marriage," Aefric said, hopefully.

"Possible," Herewyn said, considering. "If anyone is devious enough to find a way, it's her highness."

"I'm not sure that's a compliment," Aefric said, one eyebrow arched.

"Oh, I assure your grace that I hold Princess Maev in the highest esteem. Had I a sister, I would want her to be like her highness." She patted his chest. "But for purposes of this conversation, we must assume that news of her impending wedding will reach your grace before year's end."

"Very well," Aefric said. "Who next?"

"Princess Astrid of Malimfar might wish the position," Herewyn said, and the distasteful way she wrinkled her nose was adorable, and the same mannerism that Sighild had. "But obviously no such marriage alliance with Malimfar would be permitted your grace, even should he evince interest in the possibility."

"The king has been quite clear about that," Aefric said. "And I wasn't interested anyway."

"Which brings us to Princess Xenia of Caiperas."

"No," Aefric said. "Current evidence suggests that Caiperas was behind the attempts on the royal family a few aetts back."

"I had not heard this."

"I believe his majesty wishes confirmation before making this information public."

Herewyn worried at her lip. "Perhaps your grace should not have mentioned it then?"

"I was given no instructions to withhold this information from a trusted vassal."

The smile that spread across Herewyn's face then was one of the most beautiful he'd ever seen.

"Then I swear to hold this information close until your grace tells me otherwise."

"Thank you, Herewyn."

She reached up and gave Aefric a brief, but intense kiss.

"There's Rethneryl next," she said, settling on his chest again, but still smiling. "A solid ally of Armyr for centuries, and more princesses than they know what to do with."

"Let's discuss princesses another time," Aefric said. "Rethneryl, Hatay and Shachan have all sent word that they'll be sending princesses to meet me in the fall. Until I meet them, I see no point in discussing them."

"Very well, your grace," Herewyn said hesitantly. "But I trust your grace will not disregard the possibility of a princess. Marriage into a royal family will ... raise your grace's social standing more than anything else would."

"I'm already a duke."

"True," Herewyn said, leaning forward to lick his nipple. "But your grace is an ennobled former adventurer. Named for a deed and an item of power, rather than carrying the name of an old, established noble family."

"An argument I've heard most often from the Fyrenn family."

"A family even older than mine," Herewyn said through a sigh. "The oldest family line in Armyr, and they never let anyone forget it."

She grimaced slightly. "Which means we must next discuss your grace's Fyrenn prospects."

"Duchess Ashling has expressed interest," Aefric said. "And puts forth her sister Zoleen as a nearly equal prospect."

"If your grace would marry either," Herewyn said, thoughtfully, "I would think the better choice for him would be Zoleen. Duchess Ashling has an acknowledged bastard to inherit, so your grace's blood would never take root in Merrek."

She tilted her head back and forth on Aefric's ribcage. "Besides. Zoleen is younger. Ashling is about my own age, but Zoleen is hardly a season older than Sighild. She hasn't had the time or the title to help her develop the deep mastery of politics and manipulation that her older sisters command."

"I'm not sure I could trust her."

"A solid point," Herewyn said. "And honestly, a truth about any member of the Fyrenn family. They are well known for putting their blood before any other consideration."

"But you think Zoleen would be the most trustworthy of the lot?"

"She has many of the instincts and reflexes of her line," Herewyn said, frowning in thought, "but I've always had the impression that she chafes against the family reputation. That she would wish to distinguish herself as the honest Fyrenn."

"Then she's off to a bad start with me," Aefric said.

"As I said, the family reflexes are there," Herewyn said with a sigh.

"Has she tried to ... repair whatever damage she caused between you?"

"She's done nothing but. Even though I asked first for space."

"I would be willing to speak with her, if your grace thinks that might help."

"Thank you," Aefric said, and kissed her. "I'll think about it."

"Happy to help, your grace," she said with a smile. "From there, of course, we could discuss the countless minor noblewomen who long for your grace's hand, but only two of them truly merit consideration."

"Byrhta Ol'Caran and Sighild Ol'Masarkor?" Aefric asked.

"Precisely," Herewyn said with a smile.

"Now you're going to tell me why I shouldn't consider Byrhta?"

"On the contrary," Herewyn said, smiling even wider. "Of all those we've discussed so far, I consider her the best candidate without royal blood."

"Who do you consider the best candidate *with* royal blood?"

Herewyn blinked at him, amused. "I thought your grace did not wish to discuss princesses, as he had yet to meet most of his royal candidates."

"Fair enough," Aefric said with a chuckle.

"Now. Byrhta Ol'Caran." Herewyn held up one finger. "First, she's of an old family. True, the Ol'Carans are not the oldest nor most respected of Armyr's noble families, but old enough and respected enough, I should think."

She held up a second finger. "Second, her charm and beauty are quite literally beyond compare. If she has an equal in either, I've never met the woman. And those qualities would stand your grace well, in a duchess."

She held up a third finger. "Third, and perhaps most important, I am given to understand that she has done quite well as Baroness Regent in Riverbreak." Herewyn gave Aefric an impressed look. "Giving her the position was a wise choice, your grace."

"Not everyone agrees," Aefric said, recalling the furious lers who'd thought they should have been given the position. Even some of Aefric's own advisers hadn't been thrilled with his decision.

"Many might have questioned the decision before it was made," Herewyn said. "But all evidence since then makes clear that your grace chose wisely.

"She manages the barony admirably," she continued. "Riverbreak is prospering. An impressive feat, considering that its baron was banished hardly a season ago."

"A season and a couple of aetts, I think," Aefric said.

"Your grace splits hairs," Herewyn said, flicking his chest playfully. "My point is that most baronies suffering such a void of leadership would fall to squabbling and power plays. She seems to have avoided that."

"True," Aefric said, smiling. "I get the impression that the lers initially underestimated Byrhta, to their detriment."

"Undoubtedly," Herewyn said, rubbing the spot she flicked, and then playing her fingers over Aefric's chest. "Which brings me to my next point. Preparing Vercy Ol'Karmak to take up the barony when she comes of age. From everything I've heard — and my connections in Riverbreak are considerable — Byrhta is setting an excellent example for Vercy to follow."

Herewyn frowned. "Oh. I suppose Vercy must be listed among those who wish to become your grace's wife. She's made her intentions there quite clear. But am I right in thinking your grace considers her too young?"

"You are."

"Then I was right to leave her off the list." She gave Aefric's hip a squeeze. "And third, through her work as baroness regent, Byrhta has proven beyond doubt that she has an able mind for ruling, which would also serve your grace well in a duchess."

"So even though she has no title of her own, nor any dowry of note, you still recommend her?"

"Your grace has land and wealth aplenty," Herewyn said with a small shrug. "In my opinion, all he truly needs is the right wife."

"You've given me much to think about," Aefric said, tilting her chin up so he could kiss her.

"Ah," Herewyn said, smiling, and keeping her lips just outside kissing range. "But now we come to Sighild."

Aefric growled impatiently. "I trust you will not need long to make the case for her?"

"Of course not," Herewyn said, smiling wider. "Everything I said of Byrhta Ol'Caran is equally true of Sighild, save two minor details. Though my cousin is, of course, both beautiful and charming, she could not begin to compare to Byrhta at either quality. Thus, Byrhta has an edge over her."

Herewyn raised an index finger. "However, Sighild would bring to the marriage a much older and more respected family line. A value not to be ignored, and Sighild's edge over Byrhta."

"She's also a Fyrenn by blood, I understand," Aefric said.

"On her father's side, yes," Herewyn said, as though expecting this point to come up. "But she was not raised as one, nor does she think as one. Thus, while marriage to Byrhta would tie your grace's blood to the Ol'Caran line, marriage to Sighild would tie his blood to the Ol'Masarkor, Ol'Norette, and Fyrenn lines. All three much older, and much more widely respected."

"Sighild stands to inherit her own barony," Aefric said, taking Herewyn by the shoulders and rolling them so that he was on top of her. "That might be a distraction."

"A minor barony, as vassal to your grace's own Countess of Fyretti," Herewyn said, adjusting her legs and writhing just enough to make clear that she enjoyed her current position. "Sighild could hand it off to her younger brother, and devote herself to her duties as duchess."

"You raise interesting points," Aefric said.

"Not as interesting as this one," Herewyn replied, smiling as she brought her hands together someplace low.

And then they were busy again for quite some time before at last falling asleep together.

3

The next morning gave Aefric hope that the Feast of Dereth Sehk might become something like a vacation for him after all.

He got to sleep in.

Alone, as it turned out. He had vague memories of Herewyn rising sometime after dawn, kissing him and soothing him back to sleep, after whispering something about duties she needed to see to.

Aefric, apparently, had no such duties awaiting him. For a change. He got to sleep until late in the morning, when at last the servants roused him, prepared his bath, and helped ready him to face the day.

He was smiling, and dressed in a quilted silk tunic of navy blue over hose of Deepwater gray, with low, soft shoes of black leather that would be comfortable for walking, and matched the belt where his noble's knife, his belt pouch, and the wand Garram hung.

The bycocket hat with its tailfeather from a pyltenius bird went with the outfit, so he wore it as well. Even though Dajen might've frowned to see him wear any article of clothing two days in a row.

No jewelry for him today. He seemed to remember Herewyn saying something the night before about not wearing jewelry during the first two days of the Feast.

Brightstaff in hand, Aefric strode into his sitting room, where all the Knights of the Lake stood waiting, resplendent in their shining armor, and none more so than their captain, Beornric.

The knights all bowed to their duke, which he acknowledged with the salute of a noble to a knight: he formed a fist with one hand and grabbed that wrist with the other.

As he took the Brightstaff in hand again, Beornric raised one shaggy eyebrow and said, "I understand your grace had noble company last night. Shall I add Baroness Herewyn to his list of marriage candidates?"

"No," Aefric said, smiling. "She made clear that she is too happy as baroness here in Norra to seek the role of duchess."

"Nevertheless," Beornric said, and Aefric frowned in the caution in his knight's voice, "chasing the bliss moment with her was no reason to banish your guards from the sitting room."

"I banished them because I expected to take her lordship to task," Aefric said, hushing his voice so that the servants in the next room would not hear him. "I spoke with Byrhta last night. She and Vercy aren't here because Riverbreak never received an invitation."

"Your grace suspects her lordship?"

"I did," Aefric admitted, "but she persuaded me otherwise."

Ser Vria snorted a small laugh, that sent a rustle of amusement through the knights.

"Not like that," Aefric said. "She offered to wait here while I flew to Towerkeep in my *magari* and returned with the king's justiciar."

"That *is* persuasive," Beornric admitted.

"She also told me of how courtship works in Norra."

"Ha!" Beornric said, slapping the plates of his cuisse. "Sighild wants to duel Byrhta?"

"Wouldn't necessarily be a *duel*, but yes, a challenge."

"She must be *fuming* that she didn't get the chance."

"If so," Aefric said, "she's hidden it well."

"Well," Beornric said, smiling, "then please consider my objections withdrawn. While I prefer to keep guards as close to your grace as possible, no noble should face such questioning in the presence of knights."

"Unless under guard, of course," Arras said.

"Of course," Beornric said, frowning. "Which is my point. The presence of knights would have made her feel arrested."

"Are we finished, then?" Aefric asked. "I'd like to see about breakfast."

"No food is allowed until the Feast officially commences at midday," Beornric said. "Which will be soon."

"And I assume I am wanted at some sort of commencement ceremony?" Aefric said.

"Of course, your grace," Beornric said with a bow. "And for your convenience, her lordship has provided two servants to fetch for your grace through the Feast, and two porters to carry for him."

"Good," Aefric said. "I'll want to have some gifts at hand, just to be safe."

He called in the porters and servants. All four wore the pale blue livery of Norra. The two porters were big, burly men, both about Aefric's age, each of whom looked as though he could have carried a good sized tree, if asked to. The servants were small, and looked nimble. Younger, too. Somewhere close to the age of majority. One was a man and one a woman.

"What are your names?" Aefric asked.

"Alim," the first porter said. He had a deep tan, and a jagged scar across one arm.

"Parim," said the other, who wore his brown hair and beard long and shaggy, giving him a wild look.

"Kian," the manservant said. His short red hair over his dark tan made him look almost like a burning log.

"Bess," the womanservant said. Her black hair was cut short as well, though her tan was not as deep.

"Alim, Parim," Aefric said. "One of you will carry a casket of gifts for me. As this is something of an honor, and as I understand that the first day of the Feast of Dereth Sehk is devoted to games, I will give you the option. I can choose one of you to carry the casket, or you can compete for it."

"Compete," both said at the same time, which made them smile.

"These two have been competing most of their lives, your grace," Kian said. "They'd fight over a half-empty tankard of beer, to see who got to finish it."

Aefric chuckled. "Well, I can't have you fighting here and now. Wouldn't do to have you walking around bruised all day. Pick a competition that won't damage you."

"Footing?" Alim asked Parim

"Footing," Parim agreed.

Aefric frowned. He knew many tests of footing, but wasn't sure which one this would be.

Temat leaned a little closer, while Arim and Parim squared off. "The winner, your grace, will be the first to make the other fall or raise a foot from the floor."

The two porters flexed at each other, while moving their feet apart and bending their knees to lower their centers of gravity.

Arim rolled his shoulders. "Ready."

Parim cracked his neck, loudly. "Ready."

"You start," Arim said. "You need the edge."

"Ha!" Parim said, but he didn't refuse.

Instead he thrust both palms forward, striking Arim just below the ribs.

Arim grunted, but didn't budge.

Arim dealt a resounding palm strike to the inside of Parim's left thigh, but Parim didn't do more than grunt.

"Don't take all day, you louts," Bess said.

Arim and Parim looked at each other. Nodded.

Each grabbed the other by the shoulders. Started shoving first one way, then the other. Sometimes pushing. Sometimes pulling. But neither making headway.

But then Parim changed the game. He shifted his grip to hold handfuls of Arim's livery. Before Arim could adjust, Parim curled his arms inward, forcing Arim to lean forward.

Arim struck the backs of both Parim's thighs. Parim grunted in pain, but kept his footing.

Parim roared and lifted Arim clear of the granite floor by more than a handspan, then dropped him.

"I believe we have our winner," Aefric said, and clapped Parim on the shoulder. With a gesture, he called the finely tooled greenwood casket through the air to Parim's waiting hands.

Aefric turned to Bess and Kian.

"I'm afraid I can't think of anything for the two of you to contest for at the moment. But if something comes up, I'll be sure to give you the chance."

Both bowed their thanks.

Aefric smiled and took in the company. "Shall we?"

"If I might, your grace," Bess said, hesitantly.

"Yes?" he asked, trying to sound encouraging.

"It is tradition for long hair to be bound for the Feast," she said, and her compatriots all nodded. "It was the rule in Dereth Sehk's army that no man nor woman fight with hair unbound."

"Very well," Aefric said, and pulled a leather thong out of his belt pouch and offered it to her. "As you mentioned this, would you care to braid my hair?"

"Yes, your grace!" she said, and did so with impressive dexterity.

None of his knights needed change anything, of course. Only Ser Leppina kept her hair long, and hers was already braided.

"Anything else I should be aware of?" Aefric asked.

"Not that I know of, your grace," Bess said, and Kian agreed with her.

"Then let us be on our way," Aefric said.

Only three days of summer left, but Aefric would have been hard-pressed to guess that, looking up at the sky as he and his company emerged from Herewyn's keep that late morning.

The sun shone down, bright and encouraging. The sky, a richer blue today. Closer to what he'd expect from midsummer, rather than summer's end. As though the gods wanted just the right sky for the first day of the Feast.

The air was warm, but felt even warmer because it was still. Hardly a breeze in the courtyard.

The surprisingly empty courtyard, all things considered. Plenty of armed soldiers on duty — especially up on the walls — but the courtyard gates were closed.

Odd. Aefric had expected that the Feast of Dereth Sehk's commencement would begin here in the baroness' own courtyard. Was this a last-minute change because of Kefthal's unexpected appearance? Or was this just the way things were always done?

Either way, Aefric spotted Herewyn up on the walls, along with Sighild, Ferrin, and a number of other nobles. All, clearly waiting for Aefric's arrival.

"You're not late," Beornric said softly, just as Aefric had begun speeding his pace.

Tension sang through Aefric's shoulders. An old habit, from his adventuring days. Keeping nobles waiting, back then, had always been a bad idea.

But one thing his advisers had been emphasizing ever since Aefric took up his post. He was now the one people expected to wait for. To stand for, when he entered a room.

He was now a peer of the realm, and had to act the part.

So, rather than speed his pace across the wide granite path that led to the gate and the stairs up to the battlements, Aefric slowed his breathing — hoping his speeding heart would follow suit — and matched his pace to his breaths.

And as he walked, he focused on the excited murmuring of a multitude beyond the walls. The smells of enough cooking food to feed so many.

His stomach rumbled in response. He hoped the opening ceremonies wouldn't take too long.

Beornric marched at Aefric's right hand, two respectful steps behind. The rest of his knights followed, marching two-by-two, with the porters and servants bringing up the rear.

Aefric mused, wondering if he would ever truly go anywhere alone again in his life.

As he ascended the granite stairs, Aefric found himself wondering how it was that Herewyn hadn't plastered and painted the inside of that keep.

Last night, all that granite had seemed impressive. Soothing, in its way, especially when he thought of the magic involved, shaping so much stone with such smooth precision.

But now, by daylight, only a single morning later, he realized he'd be sick to death of granite by the time he left.

And he would only be staying the three days of the Feast.

As he reached the battlements, Herewyn was waiting for him. Resplendent in a long tunic of sapphire blue, over black hose, with her rapier at her side. Her long, fiery hair tamed back in a series of braids.

"Good day, your grace," she said, giving Aefric a very personal smile before she offered her hand.

"Good day, Herewyn," he said and kissed her hand. The crowd oohed approval. She then pressed her forehead to his knuckles, and the crowd cheered.

The crowd reactions struck Aefric as odd, and he found himself glancing out past the walls.

There had to have been more than two or three *thousand* people watching. All ages, sizes and shapes, though he noticed that none wore dresses, gowns, or skirts of any kind. Everyone he could see wore some kind of tunic and leggings combination.

Not just the humans, either. Aefric was even sure he saw a few eldrani in the crowd. And he counted three na'shek.

Of course, the eldrani were easy to spot because their hair only seemed to come in vivid colors.

And the na'shek, well, they stood easily two heads taller than even the tallest humans in the crowd, and wider by about the same margin. Not to mention their easily noticed skin in shades of slate gray.

All these people, assembled for the Feast. And a good many of them seemed honestly pleased to witness so simple a formal exchange between their baroness and her liege.

Count Ferrin stepped up next.

Ferrin was a short man. His skin fashionably pale. He kept his cheeks smooth, and his short brown hair streaked with blonde. But whether he was trim with muscle, or merely skinny from indolence, Aefric couldn't tell. Not under clothing so exhausting just to look upon.

The many reds and oranges of Ferrin's silk tunic and hose were simply too much. Aefric could feel his eyes tiring, trying to make sense of it all. Trying to find some sort of pattern in the chaos.

At least he seemed to have gotten the message about jewelry. More or less. True, he'd foregone the excessive number of rings, bracelets and such he normally wore. And yet, he was not completely bereft of gold, either.

He wore a thick gold chain, ending in a heavy gold pendant bearing the sigil of his county: a black bull, rampant, facing to the dexter.

Ferrin wore a longsword at his side, but his posture said he didn't wear it often. And its heavily bejeweled scabbard looked new.

"Your grace," Ferrin said, extending his hand. "I feared midday would pass without the Feast beginning."

Aefric heard Herewyn draw breath to say something, but spoke first.

"Ah, Ferrin," he said. "Always making trouble where none should exist."

He kissed Ferrin's hand then, but Ferrin opted not to press his forehead to Aefric's knuckles in a show of devotion, which made Herewyn cluck her tongue.

After all, a great many people were watching.

Before Ferrin could say anything else, Sighild stepped up, smiling brightly. She wore a long silk tunic that matched the green of her eyes, over dark brown leggings. Her so-long red hair was bound attractively in a series of braids that were wound together at the base of her neck.

"Good day, your grace," Sighild said, and eagerly offered Aefric her hand.

Ferrin scoffed.

As Aefric was Sighild's overlord, she more than had the right to offer Aefric her hand this way. But from the distaste in Ferrin's expression, he must've felt that only a direct vassal should be offering her hand to a duke.

"Always a pleasure, Sighild," Aefric said, and kissed her hand. She didn't hesitate to press her forehead to his knuckles.

Another round of cheers from the crowd. Softer than Herewyn had gotten, but Aefric noted it all the same.

"Really," Ferrin muttered.

But if he didn't like Sighild — a future baroness — offering Aefric her knuckles, the line behind her must've driven him crazy.

There were another dozen minor nobles up on the wall. All dressed in tunics and leggings. Each armed with some weapon or other hanging from their belts.

All of them likely important people, here in the barony, but none of them with names Aefric would ever even have to learn, should he choose not to.

And yet, likely following Sighild's example, each stepped up to offer his or her hand to their duke. Some of them almost quivering with excitement.

Aefric found out later that the year before, when Prince Killian had attended as Duke Regent of Deepwater, he had declined to kiss any hand but that of his hostess, the baroness.

But Aefric kissed the hand of each noble down the line, to the crowd's approval.

And by the time they were done with this, only Ferrin had not pressed his forehead to Aefric's knuckles.

From the look in Ferrin's eyes, he might have been questioning the wisdom of his little public slight. But as slights go, this one was *small*. The pressing of forehead to knuckles was never considered a requirement. Only an optional display of devotion.

But from the buzz of the nearest crowd at the base of the walls, some had noticed the absence of Ferrin's show of devotion.

Aefric was tempted to let Ferrin twist. He'd made the decision, he should have to live with the public's response.

But was an event such as this one really the time?

Aefric turned to say something to his reluctant vassal, but just then trumpeters blew a two-note rise, which was echoed by other trumpeters throughout Asarchai. And perhaps in the fields beyond.

The trumpeters sounded their two notes again, followed by their echoes through the crowd.

They sounded one more time, and all eyes turned to Herewyn.

It seemed that the Feast was about to commence.

As the resounding echoes of the trumpets faded, all eyes turned to Herewyn. The crowd grew so silent that its stirring was little more than the lapping of waves on a beach.

All work nearby — even cooking — must have come to a halt. Aefric could hear the cries of distant birds louder than anything closer.

Herewyn slowly raised her hands, spread as though to praise the gods. Everyone in the crowd did so as well, though none of the nobles or knights — or the soldiers, for that matter — up on the battlements followed suit.

She crossed the two middle fingers of each hand. So did everyone in the crowd.

She brought her hands down to cross at the wrist, in front of her chest, with the tips of her thumbs touching. The crowd echoed the movement.

"At the command of Emperor Orsk," she called in a ringing voice, "armies swept across the face of Qorunn. Conquering, yes, but also burning."

She paused then, and many in the crowd chanted those same words in hushed voices. The sound sent a chill up Aefric's spine.

"They burned temples and shrines. They burned priests and clerics. They burned the faithful wherever they could. If Orsk could not be a god, there would be no gods."

Aefric had to fight down a shiver as those words were chanted back. Something about all those hushed voices, saying such things.

"Cities fell before them. Kingdoms fell before them. Human and na'shek alike. Borog and tarok alike. All stood before the massed derekek armies and fell."

The sun beat down, and there was no breeze to mitigate it, but the day had begun to feel downright chilly to Aefric.

"People beyond counting died."

Those words were also echoed softly up here on the wall.

"Until Emperor Orsk's armies came *here*," Herewyn said, and her tone shifted away from lament to the first spark of something like pride.

The crowd's repetition was less hushed now.

"This land was not called Norra then. Nor the kingdom Armyr. But this is the ground where Dereth Sehk arose. This is the ground where Dereth Sehk said 'No more!'"

The crowd's voice rang out now with fire of its passion as it repeated Herewyn's words.

"Dereth Sehk rallied the peoples together. Human and na'shek alike. Borog and tarok alike. All came together as one, under the banner of Dereth Sehk."

Aefric could feel excitement from the crowd now, as some began shouting Herewyn's words back at her.

"Dereth Sehk gave us hope," Herewyn continued. "Dereth Sehk gave us plans. And Dereth Sehk gave us *victory!*"

Half the crowd was cheering loudly now, even as the rest echoed Herewyn's words.

She threw her hands up wide again, middle fingers still entwined together.

The crowd grew still as they made the same gesture.

"And so we feast his name and memory!" she cried.

"And so we feast his name and memory!" the crowd echoed, including almost all on the wall.

The crowd cheered so loudly then that the sound was a physical force Aefric could feel beating against his face and chest.

Herewyn brought her hands back down, wrists crossed once more, and thumbs touching.

Most of the crowd abandoned mimicking her movement, but they did settle down to hear what she said next.

"Today is the first day of the Feast. The Day of Challenges. So make your challenges well. And strive to your utmost, in the name of Dereth Sehk!"

"In the name of Dereth Sehk!" the crowd cried out, and cheered. The cheer went on longer than Aefric expected this time, and he started to wonder why.

Except that a great many of them pushed to crowd a little closer to the walls...

"And now," Herewyn said, still pitching her tone to ring out over the crowd, but turning a smile to Aefric, "by tradition, the chief noble among us must accept the first challenge. And I would like—"

"I wish to offer that challenge," Ferrin said, stepping forward.

The glare Herewyn turned on Ferrin then could have shattered good steel.

But apparently it mattered that he'd gotten the words out first.

Through gritted teeth she said — not in echoing tones, but only a conversational voice — "And just what challenge does your excellency present to his grace?"

"Agility!" Ferrin cried out. And though he couldn't project his voice as well as Herewyn, he carried well enough that some of the crowd cried the word back to him.

"You are certain, your excellency?" Herewyn said, frowning. And by her tone she seemed to be saying, *pick something else.*

But Ferrin only smiled a vicious smile back and said, "I wish nothing more."

"Your excellency knows where we stand," Herewyn said. "A test of agility here risks—"

"I have made the challenge," Ferrin said, turning that vicious smile on Aefric. "But I have yet to hear it accepted."

Beornric stepped forward. Said in a hushed voice, "Perhaps his grace should be told what the challenge involves—"

"Of course I accept," Aefric said, letting his words ring out. He'd long ago learned the tricks of being heard over the clash of battle, and the same skill ensured that his acceptance would be heard even over the crowd's excitement. "In the name of Dereth Sehk!"

As the crowd echoed those words, he said softly to Beornric, "I was going to accept, whatever the challenge was. Refusing in front of the crowd hardly seemed like a good option."

Beornric gave Aefric a grim smile, and a nod likely intended to show confidence.

But Aefric had gotten to know the knight too well to believe that nod. He could see the concern in Beornric's eyes. And Herewyn's as well.

Ah, well. Time to find out what Ferrin was made of.

AEFRIC FOUND HIMSELF STANDING ATOP THE CRENELLATION AT ONE corner of the wall that surrounded the courtyard of Herewyn's tower keep. Beside him stood Ferrin, still smiling as though this were the finest moment of his life. On his other side, the Brightstaff stood tall and secure at the very edge of the granite.

Ferrin had removed his heavy gold chain for the challenge, and allowed Aefric to hang it from the Brightstaff, for safety.

Just below Aefric, on the battlements, stood his Knights of the Lake, a dozen or so other knights, and all the nobles whose hands he'd kissed before Herewyn officially began the Feast.

The nobles stood grouped, closer to the gate, but the knights were spread out along the battlement. Perhaps to catch Ferrin, if he should fall.

For certainly Aefric's own knights ought to have known that falling presented no threat to their duke.

The many soldiers on the battlements had cleared out from this part of the wall, making room for what was to come.

The whole of the massive, assembled crowd remained outside the tower's walls. Aefric's earlier count had to have been low, because he was sure now that there had to be close to *five* thousand people gathered in the streets nearby.

And all of them stared eagerly up at Aefric and Ferrin as they prepared to engage in the first official contest of the first day of the Feast.

What was worse, the breeze had picked up. Warm, and from the east, putting it in Aefric's face.

"Your grace understands the challenge?" Ferrin asked, smiling as though he hoped Aefric would ask to have it explained again.

Once, though, had been enough.

"We move, one at a time, along the crenellations to the gate and back. If one of us falls, or even stumbles, that one is the loser, and the contest ends. If neither of us fall, we move on to stage two."

"When the spiked helmets are added, yes," Ferrin said with a brusque nod.

"A warning, first," Aefric said. "You might be tempted to touch the Brightstaff—"

"I know its reputation, your grace," Ferrin said, raising a halting hand. "I've no wish to taste its lightning, as my poor castle doors did. Shall we begin?"

Aefric nodded.

They'd already drawn lots. Ferrin was to go first on the first stage. If the second stage was necessary, Aefric would go first. If the third and final stage was necessary, Ferrin would go first again.

Ferrin held up his hands as Herewyn had, middle fingers crossed. The crowd didn't mirror the movement, but their restlessness did settle somewhat.

"I have won the lot, and shall go first," Ferrin said, doing a better job of projecting his voice this time.

"Do your best for Dereth Sehk," the crowd chanted back.

Ferrin was making a show of it, but Aefric didn't think the first stage sounded all that challenging. The crenellations were easily three feet across and two feet wide, with no more than three feet between them. True, there was the height to consider — elevation alone could make a simple task feel tricky — but overall, not very hard.

And after a couple of short steps to get moving, Ferrin made it look just that easy. Single strides carrying him from about the middle of one crenellation to the middle of the next, until he reached the gate, turned around, and came back the same way.

Aefric had already been told not to address the crowd before his try. Only the first to attempt the challenge had that right. Still, feeling the need for a little show, Aefric didn't bother with any short steps. He used one step to reach the edge of the corner crenellation, then made a light run of it, striding smoothly all the way to the gate and back.

"Not bad, not bad," Ferrin said, nodding appreciatively as Aefric returned to the starting point. "I'm glad your grace will give me something of a test, at least."

As Ferrin spoke, servants clambered up onto the wall to place large, spiked helmets in the center of each crenellation. No more easy steps, using the safe center portions.

Ferrin and Aefric would have to step closer to the edges now. Much less room to maneuver.

"What say we make this more interesting, your grace?" Ferrin asked.

"Gambling on the contests if forbidden," Aefric said. "As I understand it, we strive not for reward, but for the honor of Dereth Sehk."

"Yes, yes," Ferrin said. "Because Dereth Sehk forbade all duels and allowed only nonlethal challenges between his soldiers, who were to save their weapons for the enemy."

Which made Aefric wonder why holding the challenge up here was deemed permissible. True, if Aefric fell, he could save his own life with magic easily enough. If Ferrin fell, Aefric *might* be able to save him, but it would depend on where and how he fell…

"But I do not speak of gambling," Ferrin continued. "Only to make the contest more challenging." Ferrin nodded at the helmets. "Shall we say that dislodging a helmet counts as failure?"

"I'd already assumed that was true," Aefric said.

Ferrin laughed. "Excellent, your grace." He turned to announce it to the crowd, but Aefric stayed him with a hand on the shoulder.

"As I get to go first this time," he said, "I believe I have the honor of making this announcement."

Ferrin frowned, but nodded for Aefric to go ahead.

Aefric raised his arms in what appeared to be the appropriate way, middle fingers crossed.

He was surprised to see most of the crowd mirror his movement at once, and a decent percentage of stragglers join in.

"His excellency and I have agreed to honor Dereth Sehk further by increasing the difficulty of our contest. Should one of us dislodge a helmet, he shall be regarded as failing!"

The crowd cheered.

Aefric didn't try for speed this time. He watched his footing and hopped along. He knew he could reach the gate and back without falling. He'd done trickier things in his adventuring days, when he'd had to cross more than one unstable mountainside. Not to mention a few collapsing floors in ancient ruins, and other untrustworthy surfaces.

But getting to the gate and back without knocking off a helmet. *That* he wasn't sure about. So he moved slowly and made sure each step went right where he wanted it.

Aefric was sweating by the time he returned to the starting point, greeted by applause from the crowd.

"That was good, your grace," Ferrin said. "Better than I expected, I admit."

"Thank you, Ferrin," Aefric said, smiling at the unexpected compliment.

But Ferrin smiled back triumphantly. Raised his hands with elbows bent, in what was unmistakably a dancer's pose.

Ferrin then danced a jig across the crenellations, all the way to the gate and back. He never looked down, and he never came *close* to falling, or even to *touching* one of the spiked helmets.

He also covered the distance much faster than Aefric had.

"So this is why you wanted a test of agility," Aefric said, when Ferrin returned. The count wasn't breathing hard, or even perspiring in the least.

Ferrin smiled as though he'd already won.

"I am the most accomplished dancer among all the nobles of Deepwater. Perhaps all of Armyr," he said. "Your grace has overcome many challenges during his adventuring days, I've no doubt. And he's proven the master of several since ascending his duchy. But today, I fear, he shall face defeat."

"Perhaps," Aefric said. "You haven't won yet."

But the words felt hollow as Aefric said them. After all, stage three was timed. Speed was now as important as precision.

Herewyn began the timing clap. Quick. Steady. Rhythmic. And as soon as Ferrin took his first step, she would count the claps he needed to reach the gate and back.

There were thirty crenellations between the corner and the gate. Then there was the matter of turning about and coming back.

Quite a distance, all told.

At the starting point, Ferrin raised his hands once more. With another smile at Aefric, he repeated his jig. But with even quicker steps. He seemed to fly to the gate and back, and yet Aefric knew no magic was involved. He'd've felt it.

Ferrin did, at least, have to watch his feet this time.

As he returned to the starting point, Herewyn called out, "Ninety-three claps!"

The crowd roared approval, and Aefric applauded.

"Well done," Aefric said, sincerely.

Ferrin started as though praise was the last thing he expected. He didn't speak. Perhaps not trusting what he'd say. Either way, he nodded cautiously.

Aefric drew a deep breath and let it out.

He knew he had to get creative here. He couldn't just do what he'd done before. He'd lose, and by a good margin. Of course, he couldn't use magic, either. That would be cheating.

So instead, Aefric used memory and imagination.

There was a time, when Aefric was young, and traveling with Karbin's adventuring band, the Last Sons, when they'd managed to take down a youngish dragon that had been terrorizing local towns.

The battle had lasted ... Aefric never did find out. Felt like hours. Days, maybe. By the time it was over, he and the others weren't just exhausted. They were *done*. Wounded, and badly. Hardly able to stay awake, and debating the wisdom of sleep against the allure of finding the dragon's lair first.

That was when the dragon's mother arrived. Ancient. Vast. Powerful.

Furious.

There was no attempt at a battle. Aefric and the others turned and fled for their lives. Sheer terror feeding urgency to their spent limbs.

That mother dragon's roar reverberated through the very mountain itself. Caused their tunnel to collapse around them. Dust and rocks falling from above. Under their boots, what had been solid stone began to crack and come apart...

Aefric tried to recall that day. To imagine the usable parts of the crenellations as the only safe places to step as he fled a dragon's righteous wrath.

When he felt the fire of desperation burning in his limbs once more, he began.

Swift running steps this time. Land on one edge. Over the spiked helmet to the next edge. Cross to the next crenellation. Repeat. Faster if possible.

Aefric's mind was in the past. In that flight from death. He didn't hear the clapping of the count. Not over the race of his own heartbeat, while memory supplied a dragon's roar, and the awful sounds of that collapsing tunnel...

Some part of him must've been paying attention to the contest though, because he turned about at the gate and started back, feet still flying as though that mother dragon were right behind him.

As though her breath might engulf him any moment...

Closer and closer came the end of the race. Closer and closer, safety from that dragon.

One step shy of the door to that temple, his goal that long ago day, Aefric felt his ankle bump a rock. But his pace held steady.

He reached the end. He stood once more safely in that underground na'shek temple, where the quest had started. Too solid for the dragon to collapse. And with the tunnel gone now, no way for the dragon to reach him.

Alive. Time to rest and heal.

Hands on his knees, Aefric bent forward. Panting for breath. Sweat stinging his eyes.

But he'd survived. He'd gotten away from the dragon. He'd…

Memory faded. The sound of riotous applause reached his ears.

The warm, gentle summer breeze was what he tasted. Not coke and metal on air heated by na'shek forges. No furious dragon hunted him. No wounds to tend, save the twitching complaints of muscles from his desperate run.

Oh.

Yes.

This was just a race, wasn't it?

Straightening up, Aefric turned to see Ferrin smiling. Pointing at the crenellation one step out from the corner.

Its spiked helmed was missing.

The "rock" Aefric had felt himself bump. He must've knocked that helmet loose.

Which meant he'd lost.

HEREWYN CLIMBED UP ONTO THE CRENELLATION THAT WAS NOW MISSING its helmet. That helmet was handed to her by Beornric, who was looking relieved that the contest was over and that Aefric was still alive and unharmed.

Herewyn held up the helmet.

The crowd grew silent.

"Both men proved their agility today," she said, lowing the helmet again and gesturing towards Aefric and Ferrin. "Both men honored Dereth Sehk by striving with all that they had. Let us celebrate their efforts."

The crowd clapped and cheered. Ferrin raised his hands in acknowledgment. Aefric merely smiled and nodded to the crowd.

Herewyn raised one hand, and the crowd grew silent.

"Both men sped across the challenge field with grace and agility."

She paused, waiting for another round of applause to die down.

"I was not yet baroness, the last time anyone attempted the contest of agility on this wall," she continued. "But I kept the count for my father, and I can tell you the winner needed one hundred twenty claps to complete the course. The loser ... stumbled to the battlements in his hurry to turn at the gate for the last time."

She gestured toward Aefric and Ferrin.

"But today, neither man stumbled. And neither man needed as much time. Count Ferrin completed the course in a mere ninety-three claps. And Duke Aefric completed it in *eighty-nine*."

The crowd cheered, but Ferrin looked furious. Aefric raised a calming hand, but frowned. She couldn't be trying to give Aefric the victory...

Herewyn called for silence again, and gave Ferrin a look that made him grudgingly hold his tongue.

"But these two were not content with speed alone," Herewyn said. "To honor Dereth Sehk, they made the challenge even greater. They had to avoid knocking off these spiked helmets."

She held aloft the helmet.

"No small things, eh?" she said, smiling, and the crowd made appreciative noises.

"Alas, for all their speed, only one of our two racers completed the final course without knocking down a helmet. And thus, our winner is his excellency, Count Ferrin Ol'Nylla of Motte!"

The crowd cheered so loudly that the sound became physical pressure once again. And Count Ferrin stood there, hands held high, savoring his victory.

As the applause died down, the crowd began to turn away. Eager to be about their own contests, and win their own accolades that day.

Ferrin turned back to Aefric with a gloating look in his eye. But whatever he'd meant to say then, it died on his lips as he took in Aefric's broad smile.

"Well done, Ferrin," Aefric said, clapping him on the shoulder. "Speed and precision both, and you made it look elegant. Very impressive."

"Thank you ... your grace," Ferrin said, giving the impression of a dog expecting to be kicked any moment now. But he drew in a breath, and with only a slight grimace said, "Your grace performed far better than I expected, I must admit. I thought for a moment I might lose."

"Glad to have given you competition."

"If I may ask..." Ferrin said, letting the words trail off as though honestly seeking permission.

"You may," Aefric said, with an encouraging nod. So far this was the best experience he'd had with Ferrin, and he hoped to prolong the goodwill.

"How did your grace do that? Your grace looked as though he were running for his life."

"Ferrin, have you ever had to flee an ancient, angry dragon through a collapsing mountain tunnel?"

"Of course not," Ferrin said. "Has anyone?"

Aefric nodded. "Fleeing for my life with uncertain footing. Made for a vivid memory, to help me focus."

Ferrin didn't seem to know what to say to that, so Aefric clapped him on the shoulder again.

"Have you ever enjoyed a fall slowed by magic?" Aefric asked, taking the Brightstaff in hand once more, and returning to Ferrin his heavy gold chain, with its medallion of Motte's sigil.

"No, your grace," Ferrin said, slipping the chain around his neck.

"Join me, then," Aefric said, and wrapped them both in a spell that would see them falling no faster than leaves from a maple tree.

Aefric stepped out over the courtyard. Ferrin followed just a heartbeat behind, as though making sure this would work. But together, the two drifted slowly and safely to the granite path in the courtyard below, while the knights and nobles descended the stairs.

Ferrin gave Aefric the most sincere smile he'd seen from his vassal yet.

"That was fun!" he said, laughing.

"Your grace has never shared that spell with *me*," Sighild said, stepping up with Herewyn beside her and Beornric only a step behind. The Knights of the Lake — and Aefric's four temporary servants — followed.

"Then before I leave for Water's End," Aefric said, "we shall, all four of us, enjoy the spell together." He pointed up to the top of Herewyn's tower. "From there."

"That's safe?" Ferrin asked.

"I assure you," Aefric said. "I mastered the spell long ago. Four at once for a fall like that is easily handled."

"What about from the Spike?" Sighild asked, referring to the tallest of the Seven Great Spires of Water's End.

Dizzying, the view from the top of the Spike. This would be a fall of *many* hundreds of feet.

"I wouldn't want to try more than two at a time from a height like that," Aefric said. "And I'd have to be one of them, directing the fall, or you might end up in the lake."

Sighild gave Aefric an expectant smile.

"We'll see what we can arrange on your next visit," he said.

"Thank you, your grace," she said, and Aefric knew well the look in her eye. She wanted a kiss. But Aefric wasn't sure that was appropriate, here in front of so many. It might be taken as a statement rather than a gesture of affection.

"Your lordship," Ferrin said, looking a little more formal as he turned to Herewyn. "May I have a word?"

"Of course, your excellency," she answered, looking curious, and the two of them stepped off to one side.

"Can we get something to eat now?" Aefric asked. "I'm starving."

Sighild laughed. "Of course, your grace. But no sit-down meals today. Only what we can get from vendors around town."

"I could fetch something for your grace," Bess said, while Kian stepped forward and echoed the sentiment.

"It'll keep, for now," Aefric said. "Wait until" — he turned to Sighild — "we're out there among the crowd?"

"That's right," she said, smiling. "As nobles, we're expected to walk among the crowd, watching contests, judging, if asked, and occasionally bestowing small gifts."

"I thought," Aefric started, but Sighild paled and cut in quickly.

"Not for winning," she said, hands raised as though to stop Aefric from committing some great faux pas. "The gifts are to acknowledge great effort on the part of competitors. In fact, we are only to give them to those who lose while striving valiantly, or to both winner and loser together to acknowledge a great contest. But *never* just to the winner."

"Winning is its own reward?" Aefric asked. "In the honor of Dereth Sehk, I mean."

"Just so, your grace," Sighild said.

"Fair enough," Aefric said, glancing over at where Ferrin and Herewyn were conversing in hushed voices.

"I suspect," Sighild said softly, "he is apologizing for making that challenge."

"What was wrong with it?" Aefric asked, just as quietly.

"Strictly speaking, nothing," Sighild said. "But tradition allows the host to make the first challenge, if a noble of higher rank is present."

"Last year," Arras said, and Aefric realized the Knights of the Lake had closed ranks a bit, "Baroness Herewyn challenged Prince Killian to a contest of riddles."

"She won handily," Sighild said, smiling. "As I suspect she expected to do so again in a challenge against your grace."

"And Ferrin stepped on her fun, by cutting in and challenging first," Aefric said, nodding. "I hope he *is* apologizing then."

"Already done, your grace," Ferrin said, as he and Herewyn returned to the group.

"And accepted," Herewyn said, in tones that made clear that she considered the matter closed.

While the other nobles who'd been up on the wall for the commencement were already passing through the now-open gate and out into town, Aefric noticed that a dozen knights approached, along with a half-dozen soldiers, and a dozen servants.

It seemed that Herewyn, Ferrin and Sighild would each have an armed escort, as well as pairs of porters and servants.

Herewyn and Sighild discussed this, while Aefric looked over Ferrin's knights.

He recognized their leader. Ser Pemith, with her hard, but handsome features, her light brown skin and strong brown eyes.

Aefric remembered her as loyal to Ferrin, but true enough to place honor ahead of loyalty, when pressed by a righteous cause.

Good to see that Ferrin still held her in high esteem, given that Aefric had forced her to stand down twice this past spring.

She handed Ferrin a small pouch of purple velvet.

Ferrin drew a deep breath, looking for all the world like a man screwing up his courage, and stepped forward.

"Your grace was good enough to meet me in a challenge that played to my strengths, rather than his own. A challenge I will confess to having practiced in the aetts approaching the Feast."

Ferrin gave a surprisingly honest-looking chagrined smile.

"And despite this," he continued, "your grace put forth the kind of effort that would have made Dereth Sehk proud. And came quite close to winning."

He shook his head in wonder.

"I cannot let such efforts go unacknowledged," he said. "I know that her lordship intended to reward your grace's efforts with a gift of her own. But I have persuaded her that any reward would be more meaningful coming from the victor."

He held the purple velvet pouch out to Aefric.

"Please, your grace. Accept this with my compliments, and no little admiration."

"Thank you, your excellency," Aefric said, hoping that formality was appropriate at the moment.

Setting the Brightstaff aside for a moment, he opened the pouch, and pulled out a small statue of a black bull. It looked to have been carved from onyx, with tiny flecks of rubies for its eyes.

"Your grace knows, of course, that the symbol of Motte is the black bull," Ferrin said. "And so I come to the Feast with many small black bulls to give as gifts. Most of them are carved from ebony or blackwood. But I bring exactly one jewel, in case someone truly impresses me."

He bowed to Aefric. "Your grace has truly impressed me today. By accepting a challenge he had to know I'd trained for. By striving to his utmost. And most of all, by being gracious in defeat, even though … even though I have in the past not given your grace cause to think well of me."

Ferrin offered Aefric his hand.

Aefric kissed it.

And then for the first time, Ferrin pressed his forehead to Aefric's knuckles.

The nobles split up as they moved out of Herewyn's courtyard and into Asarchai proper. Each going into town a different direction, so that as many of the common folk as possible would get to have a noble witness their challenges. Or even judge their challenges, if victory was subjective.

And Aefric quickly learned that those challenges came in many, many varieties.

He saw footraces run both forward and backward, and while hopping on one foot. Games of throwing at targets — sometimes with knives or axes or darts, but also with small rocks, large stones, and in one case what looked like denuded tree trunks.

Wrestling competitions, tests of balance and strength. Tests of endurance and will — though Aefric found those latter the least interesting.

How could anyone be expected to simply stand and watch a handful of people do nothing more interesting than stand one-footed on narrow, often pointed stumps?

Especially when all around a noisy sea of humanity cheered and heckled other tests, shouted and laughed, ate and drank and pressed every which way.

But Aefric took watching those endurance challenges as his duty, because otherwise the only witnesses were a scant few who had personal attachment to the competitors.

Not that all of the contests were physical. Some people strove with riddles, or puzzles, or with their knowledge of history or the gods.

There were contests of painting and sketching and carving. Of music and instrumentation. Of singing and poetry.

Sometimes those latter contests involved skalds and professional musicians, but often the competitors were amateur lovers of music and poetry.

In short, if it could be accomplished in a reasonable timeframe, it was grist for challenges in Asarchai that day.

Of greatest note, to Aefric at least, was that among the seemingly endless variety of challenges, none involved weapons. Except those that could be thrown at targets.

Even jugglers weren't allowed to juggle blades or fire. Not while engaged in a contest that day.

Aefric reminded himself to ask later about the origin of this tradition. It was one thing to say that Dereth Sehk forbade his soldiers from dueling, and that they were to save their weapons for the enemy.

But it was another thing altogether to say that knights were not allowed to joust with blunted tips, nor engage in melees with practice swords, or something similar.

It was no wonder his Knights of the Lake didn't seem frustrated at spending the day guarding their duke, instead of engaging in contests.

Why, Aefric didn't see so much as a single bow or crossbow

shooting competition.

Why allow people to throw knives and axes at targets, but not shoot arrows?

Nevertheless, the air buzzed with excitement and joy. And new contests seemed to spring up endlessly.

Hardly the first hour passed before Aefric realized why he needed servants out there. He was kept so busy as witness and occasional judge that he would never have gotten so much as a bite of food or a sip of drink if he didn't have two servants at the ready to make sure he didn't go hungry or thirsty.

In fact, it was the second time that they were returning to refresh him — this time with a leg of roast turkey and a skin of honeyed mead — when he caught Bess taking a bite of the turkey and Kian a sip of the mead.

When they bowed and handed Aefric their goods, he paused them with an upraised hand.

"Are you serving as tasters?" he asked.

"They are," Beornric said, taking the turkey leg and skin of mead from them as he took over their part of the conversation. "Your grace must realize that it would be too easy to poison him here, without tasters."

"Is this your order then?"

"No, your grace," Beornric said, and though his words were easy, his expression was resolute. "Her lordship gave them their orders, and your grace will find that the servants attending each other noble today are filling the same role. The baroness would be a poor host if she allowed her guests to be poisoned by their enemies."

Aefric frowned, and looked around.

He knew his Knights of the Lake had established a circle around him, within which he, Beornric, and the servants and porters could walk unmolested.

But he hadn't noticed that they all had their weapons drawn. Held point down, yes, but drawn and ready all the same.

And he hadn't realized the watchful way his knights surveyed the crowd. As though Aefric were moving not among a crowd of revelers celebrating an ancient hero, but among a crowd of potential ... what ... assassins?

Looking a little further afield now, he spotted soldiers of his personal guard out among the crowd as well. Their weapons remained sheathed, but they were clearly watching for threats, and coordinating with his knights.

"Is this because of Princess Sorcha's appearance yesterday?" Aefric asked. "Or did you never intend to give the knights a break from guard duty for the Feast?"

"Those recent attempts on the royal family were almost successful," Beornric said. "I have no intention of allowing your grace to be assassinated on my watch."

Aefric nodded. He called Bess forward, and let her hold the turkey leg and mead for him.

Aefric's previous snack — a small, flaky, very juicy meat pie — he'd eaten while paused, so that he could use both hands, and let the Brightstaff stand beside him while he enjoyed his snack.

Now, though, Beornric's words had cast something of a pall over the afternoon. And he didn't want the Brightstaff from his hand for a moment. Just in case.

So now he had Bess hold the mead while he gnawed on the turkey leg, and hold the turkey leg while he sipped the honey mead.

He kept moving, this time, as he ate and drank. And though he continued to watch contests throughout the afternoon — judging every time he was asked, and occasionally bestowing small gifts when he was truly impressed — he also kept his own eyes roving for threats.

Just in case.

IF ANYONE TRIED TO ASSASSINATE AEFRIC THAT DAY, HE DIDN'T SPOT IT happening. He never saw his knights or soldiers so much as raise their weapons. And Bess and Kian, despite tasting everything he sampled that day, never so much as coughed.

Nevertheless, thoughts of assassins diminished Aefric's enjoyment of the festivities as the afternoon wore on. So he was more than a little glad to find himself escorted back through the gates at Herewyn's keep just as the sun was beginning to set over the cliffs that separated Norra from Felspark.

Torches were already lit in the courtyard, mounted on stakes beside the wide granite path between the gate and the tower. Aefric noted that the number of soldiers walking the walls hadn't diminished. If anything, there were more up there now than there had been when he'd left.

The other nobles began filing into the courtyard as well, including Ferrin, who looked positively exhilarated by his experiences that day. He was laughing and joking with Pemith as he came through the gates with his knights and servants.

Sighild came back into the courtyard ahead of her own guards and servants with a bounce in her step and a smile on her face. She looked so happy that the Keifer part of Aefric almost thought she should have cartoon birds twittering about her.

Cartoon birds. He couldn't remember the last time he'd thought of cartoons, let alone cartoon birds.

He found himself honestly smiling for the first time in hours, and Sighild noticed as she approached.

"It pleases me that your grace smiles at the mere sight of me," she said, giving him a teasing smile of her own, and a slight bow.

"I would challenge anyone to look upon *you*," Aefric said, "especially when you're so happy, and not smile."

"Alas, your grace," Ferrin said, joining them, "during the Feast of Dereth Sehk, a noble can only accept the first challenge of the day." Smiling, he gave Sighild a slight bow. "Though I freely admit, I would lose this challenge."

Sighild laughed, sounding even more pleased, but tilted her head slightly as she looked at Aefric.

"And yet," she said, raising one eyebrow, "I note that your grace does not seem to have taken the same joy in the day's festivities that his excellency and I both clearly have."

Aefric was torn. On the one hand, he didn't want to admit the reason Sighild was right. On the other, he didn't want to lie. Not to Sighild, as a matter of general course. And not even to Ferrin. Not right now. He and Ferrin were actually getting along, and from that curious frown, the count honestly wanted to know.

"It was the realization that we needed tasters," Aefric said through a sigh. "It turned my mind to thoughts of assassins. Made the day difficult to enjoy."

"Was there an attempt?" Sighild asked, serious now.

"Two," Beornric answered.

This news slammed shock into Aefric like a battering ram. Looking back later, he was impressed that he hadn't staggered back a step.

"But I don't believe either was serious," Beornric continued. "And both were stopped well short of his grace."

Aefric fought to school his expression. Though it was all he could do not to demand details. Or at least give Beornric a look that would warn him of a serious discussion to come.

But from the way Ferrin and Sighild were looking at Aefric, he'd been too slow to cover his reaction. Though Sighild looked almost as upset by the news as Aefric was.

"I presume," Ferrin said slowly, "your grace never had to deal with assassins during his adventuring days?"

"I did," Aefric said, managing a brief half-smile and something like a normal tone. "But I was never their target."

"As titled nobles, and titled nobles to be" — Ferrin nodded to Sighild — "we are all targets. Every day of our lives might be the day that our enemies strike."

"And we must trust in our guards," Aefric said. "I know. And I do. I have some of the best in the business. But I am still acclimating to being the one guarded, rather than the one who stands in harm's way."

He shook his head. "The transition ... is difficult sometimes."

"Your grace," Pemith said, from just behind Ferrin, "may I speak?"

Aefric nodded, noting that Ferrin didn't look surprised that his knight had spoken up.

"Your grace, my father's cousin, Ser Indith, served as a knight under Ler Klostich Ol'Ultallich."

"The Ol'Ultallich land," Ferrin said softly, "is close to both the Threepeaks and the eastern edge of my county."

"The ler was having problems with his neighbor," Pemith continued. "Doesn't matter which one. But the problem grew heated. One night, an assassin came for the ler."

She lowered her voice, reverentially.

"Ser Indith battled the assassin in the ler's own bedroom. The assassin was good. Ser Indith was ... not so young as he had been. The ler recognized that his trusted knight was losing the fight. Would likely die."

Aefric had the bad feeling that he knew where this was going. But he didn't interrupt.

"Instead of escaping to safety during the fight, the ler, wearing nothing more than a nightshirt, grabbed his own sword off the wall and rushed in to save his knight."

Pemith shook her head slowly. "Smooth as a windless lake, the assassin shifted targets and killed the ler. She escaped before any could stop her."

"And what of the knight?" Beornric asked, as though he already knew the answer.

"The knight drank himself to death," Pemith said. "Cursing himself, his failure, and his life until the end of his days."

All around Aefric, Beornric and the Knights of the Lake all nodded grimly. Sighild's eyes shone with unshed tears.

"The question isn't whether or not I understand this," Aefric said. "The question is one of retraining habits. I am accustomed to risking my life alongside warriors such as those who have now sworn themselves to my service."

"Come now," Herewyn said, smiling as she approached, arms raised. "Now is not the time for glum faces and sad stories. Now is not the time for recriminations, or worries over old habits."

They hadn't been speaking very loudly. Just how much had she overheard? Or was Herewyn so good that she *guessed*?

"The sun is low, and we have reached the first night of the Feast of Dereth Sehk."

She lowered her arms, still smiling, as she reached Aefric, Ferrin and Sighild, while the minor nobles all arrayed themselves nearby.

Aefric noticed that the only knights near him now were his own, and Pemith. The dozen or so others all stood on the other side of the group of minor nobles.

"So the Day of Challenges has ended?" Aefric asked.

"Oh, no, your grace," Herewyn said, with a knowing look in her eye, while some of the other nobles laughed softly. "But the nighttime challenges … are of a different nature. One that the common folk don't feel the need to have witnessed by nobles."

That look in her eye. The tenor of that laughter. Did she mean…

"You're kidding," Aefric said.

"Not in the least, your grace," Herewyn said with a teasing smile that put Sighild's to shame. "Your grace must keep in mind that, at the time when Dereth Sehk was rallying everyone he could, the forces of Emperor Orsk lay between us and the rest of Qorunn."

"And Orsk's people didn't just conquer," Aefric said. "They burned."

"Not everywhere," Herewyn said. "Mainly temples and holy sites. But at the time, this distinction was … unclear. So far as Dereth Sehk's people knew, they were the last humans, na'shek, borogs and taroks in all of Qorunn."

Aefric was chuckling now. "So they were encouraged to have babies."

"As many as they could, as soon as they could manage," Herewyn agreed. "And in memory of this, on the first night of the Feast, the common folk... Well, let's just say there's a thriving trade in nysta tea."

Everyone was laughing now, Aefric included.

"But we among the nobility gather to commemorate the night before the great battle. We dance, and feast, and drink in Dereth Sehk's name."

She stepped up to the front doors of her tower, Aefric beside her, and all the other nobles and knights following behind.

The tower doors were closed, which Aefric thought strange, until Herewyn spoke.

"We bring good news," she called in ringing tones. "All have answered the call. Human and na'shek. Borog and tarok. All have come, and all make ready. Throw wide the doors, that the leaders might feast one last time before dawn brings us to the field of battle!"

The doors of the tower opened. Musicians somewhere past the torch-lit entryway struck up a light, enthusiastic tune.

"Your grace?" Herewyn said, offering Aefric her arm. "May I have the honor of the first dance?"

Aefric was only too happy to accept.

Aefric had never danced so much in his life. True, as an adventurer, dancing had never been a common pastime for him. In fact, he'd only ever learned because of his time as apprentice to Kainemorton.

It seemed that the Mage of Marrisford would not have an apprentice who couldn't dance. So he'd brought in a series of dancing teachers from all across Qorunn, and simply added more lessons to Aefric's already busy schedule of trying to learn the ways of magic from a man who'd been practicing the Art since the Risen Sea was a vast valley.

That night in Asarchai though, Aefric was beyond grateful to his old master for those lessons.

There were paired dances for partners of different genders and others for partners of the same gender, as well as many that allowed for dancer's choice of partner.

There were group dances, for as few as three and as many as eight, and some that included all the dancers as part of a great, single moving organism.

Every dance had some kind of significance in its ties to the Feast.

Romantic dances representing love found during the desperate fight for life. Dances of friendship that represented new comrades in arms on a personal level. Dances of alliance that represented the coming together of unknown peoples and sometime enemies on a larger scale.

There were dances of celebration at the unity all these various peoples found under the banner of Dereth Sehk. And dances of mourning, in honor of those whose lives had already been lost to Orsk's spreading empire.

There were even dances where no one was allowed a partner at all. Each person was to dance alone on the floor, as a reminder that when the battle was over, all of those new friends and lovers and allies might lay dead upon the field.

They danced for hours that night in the great hall of the tower, taking breaks only for food and drink, when needed. But again, all food and drink were taken standing, off to the side of the hall, opposite the only chairs, which ringed the other three sides.

The food was light fare, easily eaten while standing. Spears of roast meats and vegetables. Soft, honeyed oat rolls, with plenty of butter available. Root vegetables like carrots, jicama, radishes, beets and parsnips had all been sliced into crisp sticks for easy consumption.

The drinks were light, pale red wines. Likely watered, to keep the dancers from growing drunken as the night continued.

Those chairs stood empty, for the first hour or two of the dance. No one was allowed to sit until they could dance no longer.

And each time someone finally did sit, a solo dance was called for, as though to mourn the loss of that person on the field of battle.

After Aefric realized this, he resolved to be the last one dancing.

It was somewhere around the time of that realization that he spotted an unexpected, but familiar sight. Deep maroon red leather armor, among all the bright silk and gleaming full plate. And a twirling long red braid, a shade not much lighter than that armor.

No sooner did he notice both, than the owner of that hair and armor shot him a wicked smile as she danced.

Ser Deirdre Ol'Miri? When had she arrived?

He hadn't known she was coming to the Feast, but the sight of her made him laugh happily all the same as the dancing continued.

Getting into the spirit of the Feast, Aefric danced with everyone he could. Though a few of the petty nobles sat before he got around to them.

Still, he danced with all of the knights, most of the lers and other petty nobles, and of course, Herewyn, Sighild, and Ferrin.

Ferrin hadn't been lying, either. The man was an amazing dancer. Grace, poise, style and stamina. When it came to dancing, he had all of these things, in abundance.

As the evening wore on, and more and more dancers were forced to sit, Aefric began to feel fatigue setting in. And with it came doubt that he would be the last one dancing.

Specifically, he wasn't sure he could outlast either Ferrin or Deirdre. Both hardly looked to have broken a sweat, even though Aefric himself had begun get feel complaints from his legs and lower back.

By the time Herewyn had to surrender and find a seat — she was clearly exhausted and on the brink of collapse, and yet her movements remained graceful, and her posture pristine — only Aefric, Sighild, Ferrin and Deirdre remained dancing. And Sighild hardly outlasted her cousin.

And then there were three.

With only three dancers remaining, couple's dances were not an option. So after the obligatory solo dance of mourning, they came together for group dances of celebration, of alliance, and of celebration again before breaking off for a solo dance that represented efforts on the battlefield.

Aefric made the mistake of putting a little too much effort into that one. He stumbled, which brought concerned sounds from the watchers, and several of his knights stood from their chairs, as though ready to rush in and help him.

Aefric waved them away — noticing, as he did, that many of those knights looked less exhausted than they'd pretended to be when they stopped dancing — but he took the warning from his feet as his sign that he was done.

He called the Brightstaff to his hand from where it stood waiting in a corner of the room, and claimed a seat between Herewyn and Sighild, to watch Ferrin and Deirdre dance in symbolic mourning of his loss.

Deirdre was so committed to that dance that she actually shed tears.

From there, Deirdre and Ferrin put on quite a show as they tried to outdo each other. Ferrin was clearly the better trained dancer. His movements and posture were more precise and skilled. But Deirdre had him for natural grace and sheer energy.

In the end, she simply outlasted him. Ferrin finally had to bow and admit defeat, after which Deirdre danced an extra-long dance of mourning. She moved through the room, to every chair, and danced part of her dance for each fallen dancer.

She finished, though, not in front of Ferrin, but in front of Aefric. She sank to her knees before him, bowed her head, and said, "Tonight I dance in honor of Dereth Sehk. But even this I do in the name of your grace, my liege."

Aefric was nonplussed. He had no idea at all how he was supposed to react to that.

Beside him, Herewyn blinked surprise, but began clapping. All the other knights and nobles followed suit until their applause echoed riotously in the hall.

Deirdre remained kneeling, smiling and panting for breath, even when the applause died down. She did not rise until Aefric reached out, took her hand, and drew her to her feet.

When he did, Herewyn said, to all assembled, "On the Day of Challenges, we strive in the name of Dereth Sehk, in all the ways we can imagine that were done in the days leading up to that final, fateful battle. But there has always been one quality that Dereth Sehk sought, that we could not simply represent with a challenge."

Herewyn gave those words a moment, as though to let her listeners speculate on the answer, before she told them.

"Loyalty," she said. "Dereth Sehk became the hero we know and honor because of the loyalty he inspired in his followers. And today, we have been privileged to witness a display of loyalty that would have made Dereth Sehk proud."

She gestured to Deirdre.

"Each of us tonight were dancing for ourselves, and for Dereth Sehk. And yet, this knight managed to outlast the finest dancer in all of Armyr — our own Count Ferrin Ol'Nylla of Motte — because she danced for something more than herself. She danced for her liege."

Herewyn shook her head in amazement.

"I have attended the Feast every year for as far back as I can remember," she said. "And yet never before have I witnessed such a display of loyalty. And I wish to acknowledge that by inviting you, Ser Deirdre Ol'Miri, to join us in the baronial box for tomorrow's festivities as my honored guest."

"May I, your grace?" Deirdre asked, and if there was any irony at all in her tone or intention, Aefric couldn't spot it.

"Of course," he said, smiling. "You would be most welcome."

"Then I am quite happy to accept, your lordship," Deirdre said, giving Herewyn a bow. "Thank you very much."

Herewyn turned to the assemblage once more.

"And all of you who strove to your utmost in the dancing" — Aefric noted that she gave slightly askance looks at some of the knights — "will find a small token of my esteem, waiting for you either on your way out, or in your rooms, as appropriate."

A general murmur of thanks washed through the crowd, and most of the nobles and knights began to leave.

"That is the end of the first day, then?"

"Not quite, your grace," Sighild said, stepping forward with a shy smile. "The common folk aren't the only ones who honor Dereth Sehk with … nighttime efforts."

"Then by all means," Aefric said, taking her arm, "let us go honor him."

4

For the second morning in a row, Aefric woke up alone. This time it was close to dawn when he woke, and he had a clearer memory of his abandonment than he'd had the day before.

It couldn't have been much earlier when a servant came in and woke Sighild. Aefric remembered stirring at the sound of hushed voices, and Sighild trying to get out of bed without waking him.

Little chance of that. He'd been holding her in his sleep, after a marvelous night together. Even if he might've overlooked the sudden loss of her soft, sleep-warmed skin, there was the small matter of getting her out from under his arm.

Nevertheless, the effort must've been valiant, because Aefric knew he couldn't have been more than half-awake when Sighild hushed him, kissed him, and promised to see him soon.

He must've fallen straight back asleep, though, because he definitely didn't remember her leaving the room.

The next thing he remembered was a servant — Bess, it turned out — rousing him from sleep and telling him it was time to dress.

His clothes for the day were laid out and ready. Wizard's robes of midnight blue silk decorated liberally with silver-embroidered symbols of a kind more casually associated with magic than used in actual spellwork.

No hat for today, of course, though that much black silk might get a bit warm. Why had Dajen packed *that* robe?

"It has to be the robe today?" Aefric asked Bess, who made no attempt to avert her eyes as Aefric emerged naked from the bed.

"Everyone is expected to dress as for battle today," she said, offering Aefric a dressing gown of thin white linen.

"And such robes are traditional for magic-users," Aefric said with a sigh as he donned the dressing gown. He briefly considered opting for the dweomerblade look instead — he qualified as one, after all — but there were two problems with that.

First, he'd left his old leather armor at Water's End.

Second, though he'd get to carry a sword again, he'd be expected to forego the Brightstaff.

Robes it was then.

He washed quickly that morning, and dressed, and was not surprised to find his Knights of the Lake assembled in his sitting room. This morning, Deirdre was among them. The only one in leather armor instead of full plate, and the only one of them not wearing a Deepwater tabard. Though she *had* added a Deepwater patch to her armor at the left shoulder.

She was also the only one of them wearing weapons as light as a rapier and dueling dagger. Of course, only a fool would think that made her an easier target than the others...

"Marvelous look, your grace," Deirdre said, smiling as her eyes scanned him head to toe. "Contrasts well with your grace's skin and hair, while bringing out his eyes."

"Thank you, Deirdre," Aefric said, immediately shifting his gaze to Beornric, who must've seen the question coming.

"It is also Deirdre your grace can thank for stopping the two attempts yesterday."

"Hardly," Deirdre said, scoffing. "They were just fools who had too much of drink and not enough of friends to keep them out of trouble. They hardly count as assassins, nor their efforts as attempts."

"Why would they come after me then?" Aefric asked.

"Jealousy most likely," Beornric said, stroking his mustaches. "I don't think any of your grace's policies so far would stir up discontent among the people."

"If they were even locals," Vria said, her voice soft but firm. "Not everyone in that crowd was from Deepwater."

"True," Arras said. "They might have been Malimfari, upset about Frozen Ridge. Perhaps having lost relatives, or—"

"Nope," Deirdre said casually, shaking her head. She flicked a speck of dust from her deep maroon leathers.

"What do you mean, 'nope?'" Beornric asked.

"I mean that it wasn't discontent or revenge," she said with a small shrug, and turned to Aefric. "Beornric had the right of it, your grace. They were jealous that your grace has beauties like Sighild Ol'Masarkor fawning over him."

Everyone looked at Deirdre as though wondering how she knew this. Which made Aefric feel better, because he was on the verge of asking.

Deirdre smiled, clearly relishing being the center of attention.

"I believe I have proven to your grace," she said, "that in addition to my rather significant skill at arms, I am a capable investigator?"

One or two of the knights made small sounds of impatience. But Aefric remembered sending her on a mission to Ajenmoor. How she'd not only returned with more information than he'd expected, but also caused surprisingly little trouble in the process.

"You have," Aefric said, in tones meant to quiet interruption.

"And as such," Deirdre said, "when I spot trouble, if I have time, I try to understand that trouble before rooting it out. I find that leads to a more thorough solving of problems."

She gave a snort worthy of Yrsa.

"And in this case," Deirdre continued, sounding dismissive, "I had far more time than I needed to figure out not only what these two were up to, but why. I mean, *before* I put an end to it."

Aefric frowned. "When you say 'put an end to it'..."

"I didn't kill them, your grace," Deirdre said, grinning. "The baroness assigns a certain percentage of her soldiery to town watch duty during the Feast. I made sure that the troublemakers slept off their headaches in her lordship's cells."

"Headaches from an excess of drink?" Beornric asked.

"Well, that," she admitted, before drawing her dueling dagger, flipping it in three tight rotations, and catching the handle again. "And the blows they suffered to the back of the head."

She mimed the movement, then sheathed her weapon and smiled.

"I don't believe anyone even saw me do it, your grace."

"Well done then, Deirdre. Thank you."

"A thing too small for thanks, your grace," she said, shrugging one shoulder.

"Taking down two drunken, would-be assassins, perhaps," Aefric said. "But doing so without permanent harm or any disruption of the Feast? *That* is a deed I wish to acknowledge with thanks."

"Then your grace is most welcome."

"Before we leave," Arras said, stepping closer and lowering her voice a little. "Your grace should know that the second day of the Feast is known as the Day of Battle. The day is dedicated to tributes to the battle where Dereth Sehk claimed his great victory over the imperial forces of Orsk."

"That makes sense," Aefric said, but Arras raised a halting hand.

"It is said, your grace," she continued, "that on their way to the battle, the nobles who served as officers kissed not only their own sweethearts, but anyone who wanted kissing before the battle. Noble or common alike. So if your grace kisses anyone before full sunrise, he should then expect to kiss any others nearby who want a kiss from him."

"Your knights have already done a fair amount of kissing before your grace joined us," Deirdre said with a grin.

"I wouldn't expect anything less," Aefric said, chuckling. "Anything more I should know before we leave?"

"There is one other small matter," Beornric said. "A package arrived for your grace sometime yesterday. It was intended for delivery last night, but, well—"

"Yes, Sighild had rather all of my attention when we reached my rooms."

Beornric gestured, and Wardius stepped forward, carrying a large, heavy leather book, along with a letter.

"No magic," Deirdre said. "I already checked."

"Thank you," Aefric said, checking once more himself, to be sure, before standing the Brightstaff beside him and accepting the book and letter.

The book's title was *A True History of the Great Battle of Dereth Sehk*.

Frowning, Aefric handed the book to Beornric and looked at the letter. It was sealed with a gauntleted fist. The sigil of the duchy of Merrek. But it was impressed in pale blue wax, not crimson. So it wasn't officially from the duchess, but a member of her family.

Aefric had a pretty good idea who sent it then.

He opened the letter, and began to read.

My dear Duke of Deepwater,

If all goes well, your grace receives this book on the first night of the Feast of Dereth Sehk. I hope that your grace has enjoyed the Day of Challenges, and that he emerged victorious from the challenge he no doubt faced to begin the day.

As I had the honor of first telling your grace the story behind the Feast, I had hoped to attend this year. But I place your grace's wishes ahead of my own desires in this matter.

I do, however, hold out hope that your grace will visit us at Fyrcloch. If only to investigate our vast library, and learn more of the history of Dereth Sehk, as well as any other such other matters as might pique his interest.

Thus, do I present this book to your grace with my compliments. It is only an overview of the material, and incomplete, but it makes a good beginning for the study of Dereth Sehk.

I hope that your grace will enjoy the book, and perhaps think well of me on occasion.

Yours most sincerely,

Zoleen Fyrenn

Despite himself, Aefric found he was touched by the gesture. Perhaps he had been too quick to judge her?

He shook his head. He couldn't puzzle through the possibilities. Not here and now. But he would keep this in mind, for later.

For now…

"Thank you," he said, gesturing for Beornric to set book and letter down on the table, beside the beautiful ivorywood statue of the rampant horse of Norra that Herewyn had sent after the dance. "Is there anything else?"

"No, your grace," Beornric said, handing the book and letter back to Wardius, who set them where Aefric had indicated. "Kian and Bess await without to guide us to the baronial box in the Teryrnon Grand Theater for breakfast and the day's festivities."

Kian and Bess weren't the only ones awaiting Aefric outside his rooms that morning. All twenty-four soldiers of his personal guard were mustered there.

The servants, of course, were dressed in the pale blue livery of Norra — no battle dress for them — but the soldiers were even more kitted out for war than usual. Deepwater tabards over suits of chainmail that covered from coif to leggings. Longswords on their belts and pikes in their hands.

And yet, this was almost exactly how his personal guards dressed every day. Was it the tabards that made the difference? No, they wore the tabards often when outside Water's End.

It might simply have been their bearing. Each of his soldiers seemed to take to heart the spirit of the day, and put a little extra into their movements and posture.

Aefric almost felt as though he were actually being led to war as they marched down the stairs and out of the tower into the pre-dawn.

The skies were a little cloudier that morning, and the air still chilly because the sun had not yet made its ascendance above the mighty conifers of Kerrik Forest to the east.

Nevertheless, if anything, the streets teemed with even more people than the day before. Several thousand, already up and eager to get the day's festivities underway.

And from the smells, many of them never stopped drinking last night. Not even to bathe.

Aefric found himself quite glad for the ring of knights and soldiers surrounding him. Not so much for safety — though the possibility of assassins kept his eyes moving — but because without them he might not have made it to the Teryrnon Grand Theater before noon.

The streets were just that packed.

Aefric and his company, however, had an interesting effect on foot traffic.

At the head of Aefric's group — just in front of the two guiding servants — marched a pair of his soldiers who called out every few steps, "Make way for his grace, the Duke of Deepwater."

And people did.

From what Aefric could tell, they didn't even seem to resent clearing space for him. If anything, they cheered him. A decent percentage of them, anyway. Though that might have been more out of joy of the Feast than because of anything Aefric had done to win their love.

Alcohol might've been a factor as well.

What was even more interesting, though, was that foot traffic was smoother once Aefric passed.

It seemed that after people moved aside for him, everyone heading for the Grand Theater followed in his wake. Which made it easier for those few who were trying to go other directions — to one of the other theaters perhaps, or even just off in search of work or breakfast or perhaps their beds — to make progress along the sides.

Either way, the dark skies overhead were just beginning to gray as Aefric reached the massive, oval structure of the Teryrnon Grand Theater. Truly amazing amounts of dark gray granite had gone into this edifice. Taller even than Herewyn's tower, and perhaps almost as long as Aefric's ducal castle, the Castle at Water's End, was wide.

The outside of the Grand Theater was lit by many torches in sconces. The sight of torchlight on such dark stone — especially with the skies above still more dark than light — made Aefric feel as though he were underground, on one of his old travels.

Perhaps finding some lost, ancient ruin of a civilization that might have fallen before Orsk even developed his empire, oh so long ago.

Aefric felt that good flutter in his belly. Not hunger — though that was there too — but adventure. Without even meaning to, he ignited the large, yellow diamond embedded in the top of the Brightstaff, to add more light as they approached the open doors.

Beyond those doors he could see a wide staircase that followed the curve of the building left and would take him up to the baronial box.

Guards outside those doors stood aside for Aefric's party.

As the last of Aefric's trailing soldiers entered, those doors closed with the booming finality of a tomb.

Aefric whirled. Raised one hand to force those doors open with magic, so that his exit would not be cut off if everything...

He started laughing while his puzzled knights only just stopped themselves from drawing their weapons as they looked around for the threat their duke must've spotted.

"Sorry," Aefric said, a bit chagrined, as he closed his fist and tamped down the power he'd called up by reflex. "Old habit. Nothing more."

They started marching again up the stairs in that torchlit tunnel.

So many boots on those granite steps. Even though the tunnel was more than wide enough and tall enough to easily accommodate Aefric and his knights and soldiers, still their boots echoed and echoed until it sounded as though he was surrounded hundreds of troops on those stairs.

The sound brought a good smile to Aefric's face. Reminded him of his exploration of newly renamed Castle Cairdeas, in Kivash. His knights had made much the same racket on those marble stairs.

Although the sound echoed even more here, for the tunnel was tighter and longer. The design of the grand stairs in Cairdeas was far more open.

They ascended about a hundred curving feet before reaching the end of the tunnel and stairs. The exit was guarded by two knights in full plate armor, with visors down, swords drawn and shields ready.

They stopped the soldiers at the front of Aefric's party.

"Who approaches?" one of the knights said. Aefric couldn't tell which one, but her voice was strong. A good voice for command.

Seemed like an odd question though, considering that every knight and solider in Aefric's company was wearing his ducal sigil.

As he had done in answer to such challenges before, Beornric spoke for Aefric.

"We are the party of his grace, Ser Aefric Brightstaff, Duke of Deepwater, Baron of Netar, and Hero of the Battles of Deepwater and Frozen Ridge. He has come at the invitation of her lordship, Baroness Herewyn Ol'Norette, for the festivities of The Day of Battle, the second day of the Feast of Dereth Sehk."

The guardian knight on Aefric's left bowed.

"His grace is known to all," she said, "and his party is most welcome. Be it known also that Sers Beornric Ol'Sandallas and Deirdre Ol'Miri are invited to join their liege in the baronial box. All others must either stand guard in the hall, or, if they are knights, join their fellows in the knights' box."

She and her fellow guardian knight both bowed, then moved aside to make room.

Aefric and his party filed up the remaining stairs into an arched, candlelit granite hallway. The walls were lined with pike-bearing guards, fully kitted out in chainmail and helmet, with swords at their belts.

Most of those guards wore the Norra tabard, but some wore that of Motte.

Aefric's soldiers peeled off to intersperse themselves among the other guards, as Beornric must've instructed them earlier.

Aefric was surrounded only by his knights and the two servants when he reached the arched doorway on the right-hand side, which led into the baronial box.

Beornric called the halt outside the box.

"All right," Beornric said. "Knights of the Lake, two hour rotations on guard duty. Micham. Vria. You're up first. The rest of the you may relax in the knights' box, which is…"

He looked over at Kian, who bowed and said, "Stairs down, ser knight, just the other side of the baronial box."

"You heard Kian," Beornric said, then turned to Aefric and bowed. "Whenever your grace is ready."

Aefric glanced at Deirdre, whose smile burned brighter in her jade green eyes than its ghost did on her lips.

"I am always ready, your grace," she said.

Aefric turned then and led the way past two more of Herewyn's knights — and a pair of Ferrin's, by the seal of Motte on their tabards — and into the baronial box.

Having been Duke of Deepwater for more than a season now, Aefric found that he was growing acclimated to a life of grandeur.

The Castle at Water's End was even grander and more beautiful than the royal palace at Armityr. When he was home, Aefric awoke every morning to a breathtaking view from his bedroom at a greater height than most keeps could boast from the tallest of their towers.

Nevertheless, Aefric paused one step into the baronial box that morning, his breath stolen by the view before him.

The box itself was both modest and elegant. Rather than simple granite benches, there were crafted granite chairs, with padded seats and backs for comfort. Granite braziers burned at the sides, chasing away the early morning chill, and filling the air with the pleasant scent of hickory.

But what stole Aefric's breath was the view beyond that.

Herewyn had been calling this a theater — albeit a grand theater — but truly this was a coliseum. Vast benches, where thousands upon thousands upon *thousands* could sit and enjoy the spectacles that would be taking place in the arena before them.

Aefric had never seen such a sight. Oh, as a child he'd stared up at the high walls of the coliseum in Sartis, and wondered at what went on inside.

And in Goldenmoon, he'd received an invitation to some sort of summer games at their coliseum, but he'd been pressed for time and could not attend.

Never had Aefric been inside such a magnificent structure. And certainly never had he seen one filling up with people, from the baronial box.

No. *Aefric* had never seen such a thing.

But when he had been the man called *Keifer McShane*, he had. Back in Oregon, on Earth, Keifer had attended college football games in structures that could almost compare to this one. But even those had been of steel and concrete, made with all the technical skill that twenty-first century American engineers could bring to bear.

This coliseum here in Asarchai, though. *This* was all spell-fashioned from granite. A true masterwork of its kind.

Somewhere nearby, Herewyn laughed delightedly.

"At last, I have managed to impress your grace," she said, stepping up, taking his free hand, and bowing over it.

When she came up, her smile matched her tone, but not her outfit.

No silk for Herewyn today. She wore gold-washed chainmail. Her long hair was bound at the base of her neck and her head was crowned with a gold-washed half-helm complete with nose guard. At her side hung her rapier.

"I doubt any could look upon such a sight and fail to be impressed," he said. "How many does this 'theater' seat?"

"A little more than thirty thousand comfortably," she said, still apparently delighted at Aefric's reaction. "Though, alas, we have not drawn such crowds since before the start of the wars. Today, I expect closer to ten."

"Still impressive," Aefric said.

"I should think an attendance in the neighborhood of eight to ten thousand sounds right," Sighild said, stepping up beside Herewyn.

Sighild was clad like her cousin, down the half-helm, though she looked less sure of herself in the armor.

Nevertheless, she did her best to outshine Herewyn with her smile.

"My cousin has outdone herself in planning the events of this, the second day," Sighild continued. "Word will have spread, and doubtless everyone in the region will attend, if able."

Aefric looked from one smiling redhead to the other, and remembered what Arras had told him.

"A kiss before the battle, Sighild?"

"Please, your grace!"

With a smile, he took her in his arms. She practically beamed in response. Kissing Sighild was always a joy. Her lips were soft, her tongue nimble, and she always kissed Aefric as though there were nothing in this or any other world that she would rather be doing.

And that morning she surprised Aefric by kissing him with an enthusiasm he would not have believed her capable of. At least, not in public.

Sighild was still smiling when the kiss ended, and said, "Live through the battle, my dear, that I might claim another kiss."

Herewyn — who had been smiling in approval at her cousin — raised her eyebrows at Aefric, and said, "Your grace?"

He bowed, smiling and took the baroness in his arms. She didn't try to outdo her cousin's sheer enthusiasm, but by all the gods that woman could kiss. They might still have been kissing when the sun came up, if someone nearby hadn't cleared their throat.

When they parted, Herewyn said, her voice a little throaty, "Live through the battle, my dear, that I might claim another kiss."

That must've been the woman's line, because neither she nor Sighild seemed to expect Aefric to say it. Although he wondered if there was something he was supposed to say in response. If so, why hadn't he been told?

He was saved from a moment of potential awkwardness, though, because Deirdre stepped up from behind and tapped him on the shoulder.

Deirdre had long enjoyed teasing Aefric with innuendo. To such a degree that Yrsa had recently implored Aefric to finally take the redheaded knight to his bed, saying that otherwise she'd go mad with frustration.

But Aefric had believed it was all a game on Deirdre's part. After all, a playful beauty like her doubtless had any number of men and women lining up to share her bed.

Still, there was something in Deirdre's eye as he turned to face her then. Something that said her desire for this kiss was no mere game.

As Aefric took Deirdre in his arms, she held him tight. And she kissed him with such passion that the world seemed to fall away. Nothing more could have existed than this amazing woman in Aefric's arms, and the dance of their lips and tongues.

For the first time, Aefric understood that she had never been teasing. Well, she had been *teasing*, but her teasing was sincere. That her desire for him was very, very real, and very, very primal.

Finally, Beornric tapped Aefric on the shoulder and muttered, "Sun will be up soon, and a couple of these serving women look hopeful, your grace."

Aefric composed himself and pulled back from the kiss. It seemed for a moment that Deirdre intended to fight to keep the kiss going, but she shook herself and leaned back.

She said the words, plain and simple, just as Sighild and Herewyn had said them.

"Live through the battle, my dear, that I might claim another kiss."

But the look Deirdre gave Aefric made clear that she was nowhere near done with him.

SURE ENOUGH, BESS AND TWO OTHER SERVING WOMEN CLAIMED KISSES from Aefric before he was done, as well as one of the serving men.

And Aefric wasn't the only one getting kissed. Ferrin kissed Herewyn and Sighild as well — though those kisses were more perfunctory — as well as all four of the same servants.

The count didn't approach Deirdre to see if she wanted a kiss. He looked a little intimidated by the prospect, and for her part, Deirdre didn't look as though she'd allow it.

Ferrin was also kitted for war for The Day of Battle. He wore full plate armor, also washed with gold, complete with half-helm and nose guard, and the sigil of Motte enameled on his breastplate. Instead of his usual rapier, he wore a longsword at his side in a gem-encrusted scabbard.

"I confess," he said, nodding at Aefric's robes, "today I envy your grace's wizardry. Come mid-afternoon, he'll be much more comfortable in his silks than the knights and I will be in our full plate."

Deirdre cleared her throat pointedly.

"Please excuse me, Ser Deirdre," Ferrin said with more grace than Aefric expected of him. "You're likely to be the most comfortable of us all, in your leathers."

He gave her the salute of a noble to a knight, and she bowed in return.

They took their seats then. Herewyn and Aefric in the middle of the row, with the Brightstaff standing right behind Aefric's seat. Sighild, Deirdre and Beornric to Aefric's right. Ferrin and Ler Gwalter to Herewyn's left, with one seat empty.

Gwalter had been the last to arrive, and missed all the kissing. Possibly by design.

Either way, by the time the ler entered — clad in chainmail and longsword, with a chainmail coif for a helm — the others were already seated and the sun had begun peeking over the far side of the theater.

That put the sunshine in their eyes at the moment, but Aefric suspected he'd be glad they were facing east when the afternoon heat hit.

Herewyn made a gesture with her left hand, and a pair of servants lowered an awning that came just low enough to block the sun.

She turned to Aefric with a smile. "Mustn't damage your grace's pretty eyes."

"That *would* be a shame," Sighild said, almost sounding jealous of her cousin for a moment.

Had that kiss bothered her?

But jealousy, so far as Aefric knew, was relatively rare in Armyr. That was supposed to be a major reason for the noble privilege.

A question for another time.

With the sun brightening the view around the general seating more than the scattered torches had provided, Aefric could get a better look at what lay before him.

Many of the lower tiers of granite benches were filling in with spectators from all walks of life. From fancy nobles and wealthy merchants closer to the arena itself — all armed and clad in some kind of armor, of course — to roughspun-clad common folk up on the higher levels. Some of whom carried weapons as well.

Aefric could easily believe that close to ten thousand people would be in attendance.

And down below them all, in the arena itself, looked to be the countryside of Norra, done in miniature.

The center of the arena was cut through by an arc of water representing the Fyrsa River. The dirt of the arena floor was covered with wild grass, as many of the fields around Asarchai were, and included copses of oaks and beeches, and areas devoted to local varieties of shrubs. There were even the swells of hills.

Looking down, Aefric felt almost as though he were flying over the area around this town, as it had been — or was believed to have been — thousands of years ago.

"This must've taken a full season to prepare for," Aefric said.

"Hardly, your grace," came a familiar voice behind him.

Aefric turned to see *Vohlcairna* Burrew, entering alone, and walking towards the remaining seat, to Gwalter's left.

Burrew was a woman who appeared to be some two or three times Aefric's age. Her skin was several different shades of brown, as was her simple clothing, and the two blended well enough that a casual observer might think her naked, but for her darker cloak, and thick, heavy boots.

Her face was heavily lined, and her dark brown hair liberally streaked with silver. She was surprisingly lean, considering that she projected a sense of solidity beyond even that of the granite that surrounded her.

She carried no staff. But as a nod to the mock-battle preparations of the day, she wore two wands at her belt.

"Good to see you, Burrew," Aefric said. "And marvelous work with the tower."

"Your grace is most kind," Burrew said with a half-bow before taking her seat. "And I meant nothing dismissive by my comment before, only that, for a *vohlcairn*, arranging a battlefield like this one takes no more than an aett. And only that long because of the river."

"Water is trickier then?" Aefric asked.

"I could have diverted the river," she said with a modest smile, "but that would have taken even longer, and caused other problems."

"No need to get the farmers up in arms," Herewyn said. "A simulation of the river is more than good enough for our purposes."

"Of course, your lordship." Burrew said.

"So," Aefric said. "We're to watch a recreation of the battle?"

"Among other things," Herewyn said.

"Did you actually bring in derekek for this?"

"No, your grace," she said. "We've never found any interested in commemorating this battle."

Beornric chuckled at that and said, "Unsurprising."

"They used to use makeup and costuming," Sighild said, "to give human actors a derekek look, but—"

"But that was determined to be rude the derekek," Herewyn said.

"Instead," Sighild continued, "they just completely enclose the actors in armor, and make sure their tabards bear the crossed axes sigil of Emperor Orsk. Gets the point across."

"We do the same thing for the taroks and borogs," Herewyn said. "Though we do get enough na'shek actors to represent the na'shek forces that took part."

"I might be able to get you some borogs for next year," Aefric said, thinking of the colony he'd allowed to take up residence in the far northern part of his lands. "Though we'd have to be very sure they understood this was a *mock* battle."

"It's true then," Herewyn said, frowning. "Your grace has allowed a tribe of borogs to reside in Deepwater, in the Dragonscar?"

"I have," Aefric said, in a tone that brooked no challenge.

"Your grace does as he feels best, of course," Herewyn said. "But I confess I would rather not have them here in Norra. Some wounds are too fresh."

Aefric almost pushed that point. He wanted to get people past the prejudices that had deepened during the Godswalk Wars. To help them understand that the borog armies who'd swept this direction had been under the wild influence of that evil god, Xazik the Flayer. That borogs themselves were no more evil or good than any of Qorunn's other peoples.

But he knew Herewyn was thinking of her lost husband.

It was too soon for her. And likely too soon for Norra, as well as Goldenfall. And perhaps for Motte, given the amazement he saw now on Ferrin's face…

"I will not impose them on you," Aefric said. "They are content to be mining for me in the Dragonscar."

"Is it true?" Ferrin asked hesitantly. "That they can *smell* gold?"

"I've witnessed it," Aefric said, and Beornric added, "As have I."

"Might we change the subject?" Herewyn asked, looking a little pale, which, for an Armyrian noble, was saying something.

"Of course," Aefric said. "What else will we enjoy, beyond the recreation of the battle?"

"The best way to tell you that, your grace," Herewyn said, gathering herself with a smile, "would be to show you."

She stood, stepped up to the rail, and nodded.

Trumpeters who must've been standing just below the baronial box raised their instruments and blew that same rising two-note sequence from the day before.

And like the day before, other trumpeters around the coliseum echoed those notes.

Beyond the coliseum itself, Aefric heard yet more trumpeters play that same sequence, perhaps all the way out to the very outskirts of Asarchai.

The trumpeters sounded twice more. And then Herewyn raised her hands as she had yesterday, middle fingers crossed.

The gesture seemed to sweep like a wave across the crowd, until every one of the ten or so thousand seemed to be standing, facing the baronial box, and mimicking Herewyn's pose.

She brought her hands down in front of her chest, crossed at the wrist, with the tips of her thumbs touching.

With inconsistent timing, the crowd echoed the movement.

"Welcome," Herewyn called in a ringing voice, "to the second day of the Feast of Dereth Sehk. The Day of Battle!"

She paused while the crowd cheered.

"Today, we celebrate the final battle itself. With music and dance and songs. And most of all, with a recreation of the very battle that brought down the fell forces of Emperor Orsk!"

More cheering. This time, Herewyn didn't wait for it to die out. She raised her voice over it.

"And the triumph of Dereth Sehk!"

"Dereth Sehk! Dereth Sehk!" the crowd chanted, and kept chanting until Herewyn raised her hands once more.

Silence spread through the crowd as they too raised their hands to match her.

Once the crowd was quiet, she brought her hands down and crossed them again, leading the crowd to do the same.

"So," she said, projecting her voice as well as any skald. "Let the festivities begin. In the name of Dereth Sehk!"

The crowd cheered wildly, while a veritable army of musicians came out onto the field, and began to play.

Aefric eagerly looked down from the baronial box, but the musicians were not quite ready to begin. Just as well, as breakfast was served.

The traditional Armyrian breakfast, in fact. Sliced meats and cheeses with a selection of ripe fruits, along with honeyed oat bread, and water to drink.

The meats were roasted to perfection, and still hot from the spit. The fruits — mostly berries, along with slices of apple and orange — were ripe to the point of bursting. And the honeyed oat bread was still oven-warm.

Heavenly.

"Did you know, your grace," Herewyn said, "that we owe our traditional Armyrian breakfast to Dereth Sehk as well?"

"Forgive me, your lordship," Beornric said, "but I'm not sure that's true."

"According to accounts," Herewyn said, not looking at all disturbed by the interruption, "sliced meats, cheeses, and fruits were served with honeyed oat bread on the day of the great battle. And to drink before the battle, of course, Dereth Sehk allowed only water."

"Again," Beornric said, "I do not mean to give offense, your lordship. But I've heard the same thing said of every great battle in the history of Armyr. All of them try to lay claim to being the reason behind our breakfast tradition."

"You cannot give offense by being mistaken, good sir knight," Herewyn said with a smile. "For I trust you realize that in discussing Dereth Sehk, we speak of a time thousands of years before Armyr came to be, or any of its great battles took place."

"I confess," Deirdre said. "I do find it hard to believe that *any* tradition could last after such cataclysmic events. I suspect that after the great battle, people ate whatever they could get their hands on. No matter the time of day."

"A discussion for another time," Aefric said, seeing a certain fire arise in Herewyn's eyes. "I believe the musicians are about to begin."

Herewyn settled back in her chair, and Sighild leaned in close to whisper, "Well handled, your grace," and give him a small smile.

The first pieces of the day were instrumentals, and all of them with a military sort of feel to them.

The musicians began in groups. A set of players on the lyre, before the lutes and mandolins.

Each of these were given a time to play by themselves. And then deep, booming drums accompanied them, and lyre, lute and mandolin came in together.

Aefric began to hear in the harmonies and rhythms something he hadn't expected. Four types of instruments, coming together for one song in a way that called to mind the four races that came together under the banner of Dereth Sehk: human, na'shek, borog and tarok.

When that sequence of songs finished, a single violin — standing high on a hillside near the makeshift river — filled the silence with sorrow. A sorrow shared by others, for from the lengths and breadths of the coliseum came other violinists. More than twenty, easily.

All of them played the same tune at first, but then they split into mournful harmonies, supported by a series of cellists along the river, and a soft, tapping kind of drumbeat among the hills.

They were playing for the sorrow felt by all four of those races. The many, many losses they'd all shared, as they fled and fled from the armies of Emperor Orsk, before coming together here, anchored by the land we know now as Norra.

As the music reached its lamenting crescendo, that first violin cried out above the rest — in a note of hope.

Sudden silence, save for the weeping of many, many spectators. Even Aefric felt his eyes well up, and he could hear Herewyn, Sighild, and he was pretty sure Ferrin, all sniffling. Certainly all three dabbed at their eyes with handkerchiefs.

The music struck up again, but only a set of drummers playing rough, rapid, clashing beats. It was strange enough that Aefric almost questioned it, but before he could, he saw the dancers.

They came from the far and near ends of the arena. Humans and na'shek, and two other types. One designated by cloaked hoods — the taroks — and the other by helmets with rhino horns, clearly intended to represent the borogs.

Their movements were hurried, but frantic. Desperate. Some fell, were mourned over, and abandoned, while others rushed haphazardly to come together in the center, where one, lone human danced on a hill.

Once the ragtag refugees reached that hill, the lone human stopped dancing.

Silence reigned.

That lone human — clearly representing Dereth Sehk — held up his hands, as Herewyn had done. The refugees looked confused for a moment then, tentative, repeated the gesture.

He brought his hands down, crossed at the wrist. They did the same.

And then, he began to dance a slow, simple dance.

Initially, he danced in silence. Then drums joined in. Haltingly at first, but falling into line.

The refugees all looked at each other. Fell into groupings by race. Started shoving one another. Squabbling among themselves.

The cadence of the drums broke. Clashed as the refugees clashed.

Dereth Sehk halted his dance. Walked down among the refugees. Separated those who looked close to battle. Patted shoulders. Offered smiles. Indicated through gestures that the would-be combatants should shake hands.

They refused. Turned away.

Dereth Sehk danced around them while a single, rapid violin accompanied him. Such swift, but precise movements, that even the other dancers seemed captivated.

He threaded through all four groups as he danced. And his dance conveyed both urgency and unity. And as he danced, he brought the hands of enemies together, and they found themselves shaking hands even before they seemed to realize it.

Then just as suddenly, Dereth Sehk stood on the hill again. Raised his hands in that gesture, and this time all the humans and na'shek, taroks and borogs all raised their hands in unison — as did everyone in the audience, including Aefric, Herewyn, and everyone in the baronial box — bringing them down to cross at the wrist when Dereth Sehk did.

Then the musicians struck up a slow song in a triple beat. Dereth Sehk began to dance on the hill, and down below him, all the four groups began to dance as well. And as they did, they slowly mixed together until the four separate groups became one great unit.

Then the rhythm changed to a four-beat again, speeding up, and taking the dancers with it.

Suddenly the drums boomed out a call to arms. The people scattered, taking up new positions. But still one great unit, no longer four scattered peoples.

The music shifted to a military cadence. They danced at first as though marching. But then the music grew wild, and the dancing frenzied. Both now mimicking a battle against invisible foes.

Dancers slowly began to drop, until only a handful remained from each of the four groups.

Up on the hill, Dereth Sehk pushed his dancing then. Everyone looked exhausted, but he danced as though trying to fight off the armies of Emperor Orsk all on his own.

The few still remaining from the armies of humans, na'shek, taroks and borogs — conveying exhaustion with every movement — pulled together once more.

They danced with Dereth Sehk one more time as the music built and built and built until a dancer spoke for the first time.

"They break and flee!" Dereth Sehk cried out, and the whole of the audience broke into thunderous applause.

The dancers and musicians held their dance while the applause died out.

Then the music stopped.

The survivors sagged where they stood. Looked at one another, and then at their many fallen comrades.

The survivors held each other, regardless of race. Mourned together. And then, as a unit led by Dereth Sehk, trudged up the hill to settle down.

Together.

Silence.

The crowd roared so loud it must've been heard all the way to Water's End. And Aefric cheered and shouted along with them, celebrating a performance beyond any he'd ever seen before, in this world or any other.

Following the dancing, and through the performances to follow, light foods were brought to Aefric and the others, easily enjoyed while watching the entertainment. Spears of roasted meats and vegetables. Puffs of sugared pastries filled with cream. And to drink, a light, pale sharabi with a minty undertaste that seemed to suit both the savory and the sweet.

Following the dancers were the singers. Some of their songs were said to have written in the days before the great battle itself, or the days just after.

But they all paled beside the sheer power of that dance.

It wasn't the fault of the skalds or other singers. They sang beautifully, their powerful voices full of emotion. And it wasn't the fault of the songs. They were certainly written well enough.

But there had been something transcendent about the dancers. The sheer commitment of every one of them. Even those who represented the fallen multitudes left behind by the people fleeing Orsk's forces.

They told their story with a purity and conviction that simply moved Aefric beyond anything else he saw that day. In fact, Aefric found himself pitying the singers and skalds that followed. They should have been scheduled to perform before the dancers, for *no one* should have been expected to follow such a magnificent performance.

After the singers was the main event of the day. A recreation of the battle itself. An admirable simulation of a great conflict, done in miniature. Complete with charges and retreats, desperate gambits, inventive tactics and individual heroics.

The battle took most of the afternoon, and yet it never dragged. Whoever choreographed it had paced it beautifully. All around the coliseum, voices rose and fell in time with every momentary edge or temporary falter. The crowd lamented every fallen hero, and cheered every fallen foe.

Even up in the baronial box, Deirdre and Beornric stayed on the edges of their seats through the whole of the battle. Quietly discussing this tactic and that one, what they agreed with and what they didn't. And most of all, what each of them would have done, had they held command.

So Aefric knew that the battle recreation had been brilliant. A masterwork worthy of commanding a whole afternoon's entertainment within such an arena, on such a day.

And yet, throughout it all, Aefric found his thoughts going back to the dancers. Their tunes. Their steps. Their expressions. And most of all, the way they seemed to convey so much, with so little.

It was their performance that Aefric would most remember, after his first trip to the Feast of Dereth Sehk.

THE MOCK BATTLE TIMED ITS CLIMAX WITH THE SUNSET, SO THAT A sparker somewhere near the baronial box — Aefric sensed the spellwork — could tint the late sunlight to bathe the battlefield red, as though with blood.

The only magic they'd used all day, and it created a stirring effect, rippling awe through the crowd.

A scant few actors still stood on the torn-up remains of the battlefield. Dereth Sehk, of course, but only about a score of others. Four or five each from the humans, na'shek, taroks and borogs who had been fighting alongside him.

If the mock battle was even a close approximation of how the actual battle had gone, only perhaps a tenth of Dereth Sehk's armies remained by the time they drove off the last of the derekek.

All the same, the actors roared out their victory, and up in the stands the crowds cheered them as though they'd won an actual battle.

Aefric thought about that through the applause, which continued for quite some time.

Perhaps the mock battle had been too good? Too close to real for him? Was that why he preferred the dancing?

After all, Aefric had seen more than his share of battles during the Godswalk Wars. Perhaps he had seen too much of the real thing to appreciate a facsimile. Whereas the dancers had focused on the emotions of their efforts, rather than on weapon work, and tactics.

Something for him to think about, during the ride back to Water's End.

But that ride would not come for two days yet. And right now the applause was finally dying down, and Herewyn was standing once more. Hands raised in the manner of Dereth Sehk.

Slowly, the pose spread through the crowd, until enough had followed suit that all were giving her their attention.

She lowered her hands and crossed them.

"The battle is over!" Herewyn called out to the crowd. "The day is won. And now we feast and drink and dance in the name of Dereth Sehk!"

"In the name of Dereth Sehk!" the crowd half-chanted half-yelled back, and then gave one more wild cheer before they began filing out toward the exits.

Herewyn turned back to Aefric, smiling.

"Your grace," she said. "As the ranking noble present in Asarchai today, tradition presents your grace a choice. He is welcome to go out among the common folk and celebrate, as some say Dereth Sehk did following the battle. Or he is welcome to come celebrate with the nobles, for others say Dereth Sehk celebrated with his officers, who all came from the nobility."

"Sources vary," Sighild said, suppressing a giggle.

"They do," Herewyn said. "However, if scholarship matters in this, there is more evidence that Dereth Sehk's priority following his great victory was working with the leaders of his remaining forces. And thus, the nobles."

"And yet," Ferrin said, "there *is* convincing evidence that he went first among the people, where he was said to feel most at home, and celebrated with them before returning to the nobles the following day."

"As has been established," Herewyn said, "sources vary. Which is the reason that tradition offers your grace a choice."

Herewyn cocked an eyebrow at Aefric. "Then again, given what I have seen of your grace, I suppose he might do one, and then the other."

"If your grace *does* wish to do both," Ferrin said, frowning, as though he might actually be concerned, "I would personally suggest your grace go first among the common folk. Before their celebrations risk … becoming excessive, and they lose sight of the importance of your grace's person."

"If I may, your grace," Beornric said.

Aefric suppressed a sigh, but nodded for his knight-adviser to go ahead.

"There have already been two attempts on your grace's life—"

"*What?*" Herewyn snapped, apparently only just learning this.

"His knights *say* they weren't serious," Sighild said. "But after the attacks on their majesties—"

"It's all right, Sighild," Aefric said. "Herewyn. It's not as bad as it sounds." He turned to Deirdre. "If you would."

"Of course, your grace," Deirdre said, and waited until she had everyone's attention to continue. "They were not assassins. Just drunken louts. Jealous that among his grace's considerable gifts are the affections of noble beauties such as yourselves."

Sighild blushed a pretty shade of pink.

"I assure you," Deirdre continued. "Rendering them both unconscious was the work of no more than a moment. And they rest now in her lordship's cells, no threat to anyone. Except themselves, of course."

"That is all true," Beornric said. "And yet it occurs to me that, were I an assassin, I would enflame the jealousies of just such drunken louts, that they might give me a look at his grace's defenses."

"Let them look," Deirdre said, smiling. "It won't help."

The Deadly Feast

"So you think the threat remains," Sighild said, to Beornric.

"The threat is always there," Ferrin said. "For each of us."

That wasn't what Beornric meant, and Aefric knew it.

"You think there *is* an assassin in town?" he asked.

"I think we would be fools to assume there isn't one," Beornric said. "Especially after Kefthal's strange appearance. Therefore, it is my formal request, as your knight-adviser and the captain of your personal guard, that your grace restrict his celebrations to her lordship's feast tonight, where we'll have an easier time ensuring your grace's safety."

"You know I'm not fond of hiding," Aefric said.

"Hiding from what, your grace?" Beornric asked. "No formal threat has been issued. Your grace has a choice of parties, and I am requesting that he choose the safer option."

Aefric could practically hear Beornric adding, "The noble's choice, rather than the adventurer's choice." Aefric sighed at that subtext, but he did feel grateful that Beornric didn't say the words aloud. Not here in front of so many others.

"Please, your grace," Herewyn said. "The common folk saw a great deal of their duke yesterday afternoon. But last night, we were all so involved in the traditional dances that your grace had little time for socializing among the nobility."

Sighild gave him a big-eyed look and opened her mouth to add what would doubtlessly be her own request that he forgo celebrating with the common folk.

"All right," Aefric said, getting the words out before Sighild — or anyone else, for that matter — could beat him to it. He wasn't sure he'd intended to go out into town anyway. He turned to Herewyn. "I would be most delighted to celebrate with your lordship and the nobility at your keep this evening."

"Thank you, your grace," she said with a smile and a small bow. "There is, of course, time for us all to freshen up beforehand. As well as change out of our armor, and dress for a celebration."

"Thank the gods," Ferrin muttered.

He must've said that louder than he intended. Because while the nobles all chuckled in response, he gave a chagrined smile.

"Full plate holds the hot sun better than I remembered," Ferrin said.

"Then by all means," Herewyn said, "let's get out of the dregs of that sunlight and into more forgiving clothing."

With that — and Aefric's group leading the way — they made their way out of the coliseum.

AEFRIC TOOK FULL ADVANTAGE OF HEREWYN'S PROMISE OF TIME TO freshen up. He lingered in his bath, and really enjoyed the enchantments that Burrew had lain on that smooth, granite tub.

Soaking in hot water scented with fennel. A pure delight.

Aefric hadn't sweated as much as those in heavier armor that day, but the day had still been long and involving.

Especially the dancing, which Aefric found himself thinking about again as he bathed. He would have to try to convey the sheer brilliance of it in his next letters to Byrhta and Maev, but he knew he'd fall short.

He might have to settle for conveying his reaction, and hoping that made up the difference.

After the bath, he considered his outfit. He was to dress for a celebration, but Herewyn hadn't been clear how *formal* a celebration.

Informal, he decided. After all, this was the Day of Battle. Chances were that the party the survivors threw back then hadn't been heavy on formality.

Of course, the nobles *had* celebrated separately from the common folk...

Assuming that was true, and not ... historical license.

Yes. Informal. So he wouldn't wear the Deepwater colors, but something a little flashier.

And, of course, Dajen had packed him options.

Aefric settled on a sky blue tunic over cream-colored hose, with a cloth-of-gold sash belt suspending his noble's dagger, belt pouch and the wand Garram, and soft shoes of gold-leafed pale leather.

The tunic was a little fancier that his usual. This one had pearl buttons, and interesting designs embroidered at the cuffs and collar.

He wore his sandy blonde hair down, free past his shoulders. Deciding that jewelry was probably expected, he adorned himself with the emerald ring Queen Eppida had given him, along with a gold chain suspending a large sapphire that had been cut to the shape of Lake Deepwater.

The Brightstaff, of course, completed the outfit.

For a change, when Aefric emerged into his sitting room, only a handful of knights awaited him.

Ser Beornric, of course, wearing a rust-brown doublet over a tunic the color of parchment, and dark brown hose. As a knight, he still wore his longsword at his side, but to Aefric's surprise the older knight actually wore a little jewelry. A golden oak tree, pinned to his doublet.

The other two knights were Leppina and Temat, both of whom still wore their full plate. Clearly, they'd drawn guard duty tonight.

"Anything I need to know before we head down?" Aefric asked.

"If so," Beornric said, "they've neglected to tell me."

"Probably not, then," Aefric said, chuckling. He pointed out the golden oak tree. "A gift from his majesty?"

The royal sigil was a golden oak tree on a field of forest green.

"Yes, your grace," Beornric said, puffing out his chest just a little. "In commemoration of my years of service to the crown, before he allowed me to enter into your grace's service."

"And I'm lucky he did," Aefric said, clapping his knight-adviser on the shoulder. "Shall we?"

Kian and Bess were waiting again in the hall, and escorted Aefric and his knights down those smooth, granite stairs into the great hall, which was set for a feast.

And quite a feast. It looked as though every ler and knight in Norra — and more than a few from the surrounding baronies and counties — were in attendance. Enough people to fill more than a dozen tables, and that didn't include the baroness' table up on the dais, at the far end of the hall, where seating for eight awaited.

And everyone in the hall seemed to be dressed for celebration, wearing bright colors and flashing a great deal of jewelry. Even the knights, who were most easily spotted by the weapons dangling from their belts.

As Aefric entered the room, he was announced by a herald. Everyone who had been sitting, stood.

This, in and of itself, was nothing new to Aefric. And yet, seeing so very many people all stop their easy conversation and laughter to stand for him still sent a little chill up his spine.

How much worse must it be for the king? Whose court was likely this size every night?

As Aefric was led through the tables by Kian and Bess, with Beornric at his side and Leppina and Temat following, the crowd of knights and nobles bowed as Aefric passed.

He was pleased to note his off-duty Knights of the Lake scattered among the tables, all dressed in their finery.

He reached the dais, where he was grateful to realize that he was not the last to arrive. Herewyn was not here yet, which he considered right and proper. These were her lands, after all, and this her party. She should get to make the grand entrance.

Several others *were* already on the dais, though.

Aefric's eyes went first to Sighild who wore a turquoise blue gown, with sleeves and skirts slashed with crimson. She wore bracelets of woven gold, and her low neckline was highlighted by a pendant that mixed rubies and pale sapphires in an interesting design.

She wore her shimmering red hair in a long twist, kept in place by some kind of woven gold.

Chatting with Sighild — and apparently having trouble keeping his gaze above her neckline — was Count Ferrin, who wore a tunic of cloth-of-gold over silver hose.

The man's tunic was so shiny that Aefric couldn't actually tell at first if he was wearing any additional jewelry.

He probably was. He seemed to favor excess that way.

Also involved in the conversation were Ler Gwalter, dressed in bright reds and blues, Ser Pemith, who favored dark greens and browns, and a woman Aefric didn't know.

That woman had pale brown skin, and long, dark curly hair. She wore a gown of bright orange in a shade that suited her skin tones, slashed here and there with canary yellow. She wore gold rings on two fingers — one anchored by a ruby, the other a garnet — and a necklace of thick gold.

"Your grace," Ferrin said, inviting Aefric and Beornric to join the conversation while Leppina and Temat did their best to fade into the background, like the other guards Aefric noted here and there around the perimeter. "I don't believe you've met Ler Onoalla Ol'Errekre."

"I am most pleased to meet your grace," the newcomer said with a bow, "about whom I have, of course, heard a great deal."

"The pleasure is mine, Ler Onoalla," Aefric said, offering a slight bow in return. "And this is Ser Beornric Ol'Sandallas, one of my most important advisers."

"Ler Onoalla," Ser Beornric said with a bow, while she saluted him by making a fist and grasping the wrist behind it.

"Was just telling his excellency and the others," Onoalla continued, "that I hated to miss so much of the Feast, but I was delayed in the south."

"Nothing too serious, I hope," Aefric said.

"More of an irritation than a real problem," she said with a small smile. "And surely nothing that would require your grace's attention."

Before Aefric could ask — because that answer had made him only more curious — the baroness was announced.

The attention of the room shifted to the entryway, and Aefric realized that no one had resumed sitting yet.

Did they stay standing while waiting for the baroness? Would they not be allowed to sit until she did? Or perhaps not until Aefric did?

These were the smaller details of life as an Armyrian noble that Aefric had yet to master.

In any event, Herewyn made quite an entrance.

She was dressed in a gown of vivid purple silk, slashed at the sleeves and skirts with burnt orange lace. She wore a pair of gold bracelets on each wrist, and a delicate gold chain around her neck that ended in a piece of jewelry that combined amethysts and citrines.

She wore her long, shimmering red hair down, draped around her shoulders.

All eyes stayed on Herewyn as she moved through the room, acknowledging bows and salutes with a smile here and a word there.

As she ascended the steps to the dais, she gave Aefric a broad smile and said, "As all of Norra is yours, your grace, I offer my liege his choice of seats. If your grace wishes the head of the table for the celebration on the Day of Battle, I am more than happy to cede it to him."

"Some would say that the seat properly belongs to Dereth Sehk," Gwalter said softly, "who might be most appropriately represented by your grace."

Aefric shook his head with a smile that matched the baroness'. Though her words had been conversational, he let his voice project as he replied.

"It is your lordship who has brought us all together. Your lordship who has made all the arrangements for not only the great battle, but what I am sure will be an excellent celebration to follow. If any of us could be said to hold the role of Dereth Sehk today, I would say it is your lordship."

Herewyn looked astonished, and more than a little moved by Aefric's words, while cries of agreement sounded around the hall.

"Well, then," she said, bowing to Aefric, "it shall be as your grace suggests. And I trust he will consent to sit at my right hand?"

"It would be my honor," Aefric said.

They took their seats then. Sighild to Aefric's right, and Ferrin straight across from him. Across from Sighild sat Onoalla, then Beornric and Pemith, with Gwalter sitting at the foot of the table.

Musicians in one corner of the room struck up a jaunty tune, and the feast was ready to begin.

THE FEAST ITSELF, AEFRIC WAS TOLD, WAS BASED ON WHAT HISTORIANS believed the people actually ate in celebration, following the great battle. So instead of several courses full of delicate flavors that showcased the skills of the local chefs, the meal was simple.

Boar steaks, roasted together with spices and root vegetables. Served with oat bread that was heavy on the honey, because historians insisted that the refugees had no cattle, and thus, no butter.

And to drink, lots of mead. Not a sweet mead, though, but one brewed with a spicy tang reminiscent of cinnamon.

For dessert, apple pie, which was likely far flakier and crispier than anyone had been up to baking in the hours following the actual battle.

But Aefric wasn't one to quibble.

Conversation over dinner was simple, and focused largely on Dereth Sehk. Especially — and this was a lively discussion that took most of the meal — the question of whether or not any kindaren had taken part in the battle.

According to Herewyn, sources conflicted, so every three years they were given representation — proportional to the number of scholars who insisted that the kindaren had, indeed taken part in the battle.

Ferrin and Gwalter, however, both argued strenuously that kindaren had played a key role. And that a kindaren named Elsinet had been a key adviser to Dereth Sehk, and that her exclusion from the festivities was just this side of criminal.

Sighild supported her cousin, and the argument grew heated. Both sides flung the names of scholars back and forth like weapons.

Aefric, surrounded entirely by the argument — and he was pretty sure he heard it carry on to other tables down below the dais — simply lacked the frame of reference to keep up, let alone participate.

At least, until old memories surfaced...

Back on Earth, in another lifetime, he had known the world of Qorunn only through the roleplaying game sourcebooks of *The Torn Kingdoms*, supposedly created by Del Baker.

He had remembered from those books that Dereth Sehk played a role in the history of this part of the continent. But since that era had been thousands of years before what Keifer McShane had thought of as "the playable era," he'd only ever skimmed it.

But something about this argument made him remember more.

The story of Dereth Sehk had been around since the first edition of *The Torn Kingdoms Campaign Setting*. But it had changed in the third edition. The story as presented in the third and fourth editions of the setting included kindaren among the armies gathered by Dereth Sehk.

But when fifth edition came out, some continuity editor noticed a timeline problem between the first appearances of kindaren in the setting and the Great Victory of Dereth Sehk.

Kindaren were excluded again.

Sixth edition was due to come out, back on Earth. If it hadn't come out already. Aefric didn't know if there was a time differential between Earth and Qorunn.

Were all of these people around him debating a historical point because of inconsistencies in previous editions of the game? Or was the question arising because kindaren were being added back to the armies of Dereth Sehk in the sixth edition, and so new information would soon come to light, confirming the kindaren role in the battle?

Or was it the other way around? Did the editions of the game vary because of the work of conflicting scholars on Qorunn?

Aefric found himself wondering once more just what the relationship was between Qorunn, the actual world he now lived in, and Qorunn, the setting of a roleplaying game on Earth.

And just what role did Del Baker, "creator" of *The Torn Kingdoms*, play in all this?

Aefric was pondering all of this through dessert — while the argument had been flowing steadily the whole time — but suddenly realized that everyone at the table was looking at him, expectantly.

"Your grace?" Herewyn said.

"Forgive me," Aefric said. "I've done my best to follow all of the arguments and citations and quotations from various sources. But if you are expecting me to settle the issue, I'm afraid I can't."

"Your grace has no opinion then," Ferrin said, "on the presence of kindaren among the armies of Dereth Sehk?"

"Dereth Sehk was, I fear, only a vague name to me just a season ago." He smiled at the surprised looks on several faces. "You must all remember that I'm from Sartis originally. And though I've traveled far and wide, I spent little time around Armyr until late in the Godswalk Wars."

"They speak little of Dereth Sehk down in Sartis, then?" Onoalla asked.

"Not at all," Aefric said, shaking his head. "They give their attention to their own heroes down there."

"As they should," Herewyn said, smiling. She raised her glass of mead. "To all the heroes from every corner of Qorunn. Historians may dispute their details, but we all owe them great thanks for their deeds."

"To the heroes!" Aefric echoed, raising his goblet in confirmation.

The call was echoed around the hall, and everyone drank.

"And perhaps by the next feast," Herewyn said with a teasing tone, "your grace will be expert enough to enter into the kindaren debate?"

"Perhaps," he said, smiling. "But I wonder if it is wise to resolve the question. After all, you would no longer have your lively debate. An annual event, I presume?"

"A tradition unto itself," Sighild said, but Ferrin laughed approvingly.

"Your excellency?" Herewyn asked.

"Your grace is too subtle," Ferrin said, smiling. He turned to Herewyn. "His grace just implied that if he turns his attention to the study of Dereth Sehk, by the next Feast he would not only develop his own opinion, but resolve the very question of kindaren involvement itself."

"Here, here," Gwalter said, toasting Aefric, while Beornric and Pemith both exchanged glances and hid behind reserved smiles. Onoalla and Sighild both raised their eyebrows at Aefric. And Herewyn chuckled as she turned to him.

"I will admit that, as a wizard, your grace has likely spent more time at study than everyone else at this table combined," Herewyn said. "But I trust even a brief exposure to this debate makes clear to your grace that the nobility of Norra" — she nodded to Ferrin — "and Motte" — she turned back to Aefric — "have devoted considerable attention to the matter through the years."

"I do not wish to impugn the efforts of any, let alone my hostess and her esteemed guests," Aefric said. "I do not know that I would be able to resolve this question, even if I should have as much time to research the matter as I would like."

"Which you won't, your grace," Beornric said. "I can almost promise that."

"I mean only that the years have taught me that I approach scholarship differently than most. While I have no doubt that all of you have done a great deal of focused research on Dereth Sehk, his battle, and the times and events around it, I myself would approach the question differently."

"How?" Hereyn asked, cocking her head curiously.

"Oh, don't answer, please, your grace," Ferrin said with a sly smile. "Let us all be amazed by your grace's discoveries at the Feast next year."

This was a trap. Aefric had been an adventurer too long not to recognize one when he saw it.

But some traps were worth springing, so he smiled as he answered.

"Very well, then. I shall do such research as I can over the coming year, and present on my findings at next year's Feast."

"I look forward to hearing the results," Herewyn said, her voice somewhere between cautious and curious.

Aefric looked forward to that himself.

One year of research, to answer a question that had clearly been debated for decades. Perhaps longer.

And an even deeper question than that.

Would Aefric's research here in Qorunn affect the answer published in the sixth edition of *The Torn Kingdoms Campaign Setting* on Earth? Or would Del Baker's choices in publishing the campaign setting affect the outcome of Aefric's research?

That was the question he truly wanted answered. If only he could think of a way to *get* that answer.

But Herewyn distracted Aefric from such thoughts by standing. No need for special hand signs here in the great hall of her own keep. When the baroness stood, all eyes turned to her and conversations around the hall died out.

"Last night," she said, "this hall was transformed by our dancing into a place of tribute. And while it would be easy enough for the servants to clear away the tables and chairs for a grand ball, this year I have something better in mind."

She paused, while the crowd murmured speculations about what the baroness might be planning.

"Now," she said, getting the hall's attention again. "In the past, we have sometimes used three smaller halls for our dancing following the Day of Battle." She tossed her hair slightly. "And I believe some of you made interesting use of the alcoves."

There were murmurs of amusement all around.

"But this year, in honor of the first attendance of our new duke, I thought we would do something different."

She clapped her hands, and a series of pages came in, one approaching each table, while the eldest — a dark young man who had to be close to his majority — approached the baronial table.

"If you would all please follow your pages," Herewyn said. "They know the order in which to lead you."

There was the sound of over a hundred chairs scraping their legs back over the granite floor as people began to stand and file out — accompanied by a good deal of lively speculation — to see what their baroness had planned.

"Noble guests," the senior page said, addressing Aefric and the others at the baronial table, "as we have a moment before it is our turn to leave, may I call for anything? More food or drink, perhaps?"

"Ishka," Herewyn said, smiling. "I think we should all drink a toast, before we adjourn to the dancing."

The senior page gestured to the servants, and a bottle of ishka was brought forth, along with several small silver cups. A measure of brown liquor was poured into each of the cups, which were handed out to Herewyn and her guests.

She stood, not yet raising her cup.

"As this is the Feast of Dereth Sehk," she said, "I know it is expected that we drink to him." She gave a conspiratorial smile then. "But technically we are between events, and I wish to take advantage of that for a different toast. Do we have any objections?"

No one at the table spoke up against her plan.

"Excellent," she said, and raised her cup. "To all the heroes of the Godswalk Wars. To those living" — she nodded to Aefric — "and those who gave their lives for others. May their efforts and their sacrifices buy us a thousand years of peace and prosperity."

"Here, here," Gwalter said, standing and raising his cup in confirmation.

All around the table, then, everyone stood and raised their cups in confirmation of the toast.

As one, they drank.

The ishka was strong enough to burn on its way down, but its taste was full and rich, with a hint of almonds.

"Mountain Home ishka?" Aefric asked.

"The best in all Armyr," Herewyn said with a smile.

The room was almost completely clear by then, and the senior page stepped up and said, "Your grace, your lordship, your excellency, and all true knights and lers, the way is prepared."

"Excellent," Herewyn said. "By all means. Lead us to the dance!"

THE SENIOR PAGE LED AEFRIC AND THE OTHERS UP TO THE ROOF, WHERE servants had done a great deal since the night of Aefric's arrival in Asarchai.

The raised platform in the middle was now a small banquet, where drinks and more food were available, in case anyone didn't get enough at dinner.

The edges of the roof were lined with tall, thick bushes, laden with dark red berries, that sweetened the air with a fresh, somewhat familiar scent.

Then Aefric recognized those berries from his travels. He'd never learned the official name for them, but he knew that they were juicy and had a sweet, tangy taste that swept the mouth clean after only … a few swallows…

He chuckled. Breath fresheners.

The bushes that lined the perimeter — and there were more that created private nooks and alcoves here and there, as well as what looked like a small maze — all that same type. So wherever people went on the roof, breath fresheners would be within easy arm's reach.

Kind of went with the mood lighting.

The skies were clear, with only a sliver of moon. So most of the light came from soft, twinkling yellow lights that flitted about, brightening the night to a comfortable dimness that suggested intimacy.

Illusions, of course, those flitting lights. Burrew's work, which suggested that during her apprenticeship she had, indeed, studied at least a *few* spells outside of the magic of clay and stone.

But it was her mastery of the magic of clay and stone that was holding onto the day's heat, and keeping the roof of the keep comfortably warm.

The other nobles and knights had already arrived and begun scattering about into smaller groups, talking among themselves as they awaited the arrival of the baroness' party.

At Herewyn's nod, the musicians — stringed groups scattered here and there, which made Aefric wonder how they coordinated — struck up a series of notes that grabbed everyone's attention.

"Your grace," Herewyn said, turning to Aefric with a slight bow, "would you do me the honor opening the dance with me?"

"The honor would be mine, your lordship," Aefric said. And he tossed the Brightstaff into the air. At his will it flew over the crowd to stand on one corner of the platform, both out of the way, and still near at hand.

The musicians struck up an Errantor rhythm then, which was a style of dancing where the women led and the men followed.

Herewyn led well, and kept Aefric moving and turning smoothly around the roof. And everywhere they danced, more couples began to join in.

"I don't know how you do it, Herewyn," Aefric said, as she gently spun him three times in place, before taking his waist and getting them moving once more.

"Do what, your grace?" she asked, smiling and changing directions exactly on the beat.

"You move with such refinement and ease that I feel like a clumsy ogre beside you. And yet, dancing, you make me *feel* graceful."

"Your grace is too kind," she said, then lowered her voice. "And you exaggerate. You've obviously had training."

"I'm not talking about training," he said. "What I'm talking about can't be taught. It is a gift for movement from the gods themselves."

Herewyn's cheeks actually flushed a soft pink.

"Such compliments," she said softly. "I might think your grace intends to invite me to his rooms tonight."

"I doubt anyone could dance with you and not be tempted," Aefric said.

The music came to a crescendo, and Herewyn dipped Aefric. For a moment, he thought she would kiss him. Instead, she smiled teasingly, and pulled him back to a standing position.

"If your grace invites me," she said softly, "I shall be most happy to accept." She put one hand on his chest. "But I think my other noblewomen — to say nothing of my dear cousin — would accuse me of monopolizing your grace's attentions."

Before Aefric could reply, Herewyn turned away to dance with one of her nobles.

He chuckled and turned, to find one of his own knights standing before him.

Vria. Small and pale, with golden eyes, hints of orange in her hair, and the perfection of features that left no doubt that some of her heritage was eldrani.

She wore a simple, elegant gown of cobalt blue and adorned only one piece of jewelry. A cameo on a delicate golden chain.

"Will you dance with me, Vria?" Aefric asked.

"I would like nothing better, your grace," Vria said with an impressively dazzling smile.

After Vria he danced with Sighild, and then Onoalla, and Deirdre — who looked stunning in a gown of forest green — and then he began to lose track. Every time a song ended, there were women around who wanted the next dance. And Aefric felt it was his obligation, as duke, to dance with as many as he could.

Still, after a couple of hours of dancing, he was more than a little grateful when Sighild suggested a small walk, rather than a dance.

They made their way along the perimeter, arm-in-arm, and she was quick to steer them into the first nook they came across.

It was quite nice in there. Private, with a wooden bench that looked fairly comfortable.

"A wooden bench," Aefric said with a smile, gesturing for Sighild to sit. "It's a wonder Burrew allowed it."

"I think my cousin overruled her," Sighild said, smiling as she sat. "With your grace in attendance, she's been looking at the décor afresh, and thinking it may be time for floorboards and plaster. If only here and there, for variety."

"I agree," Aefric said, sitting beside her. "Are you enjoying the dancing?"

"I am," she said. "Though your grace is in sufficient demand that I began to think the night would end before I had another moment of his time."

"I am the senior noble at the dance," Aefric said, shrugging one shoulder. "Of course they want to dance with me."

Sighild cocked an eyebrow. "And how many of these noblewomen made clear their interest in sharing the noble privilege with your grace tonight?"

"Likely about as many as the noblemen who made similar offers to you," Aefric said. "And isn't that the point of the noble privilege? To encourage the pursuit of bliss and discourage jealousy?"

"Yes, your grace," she said with a slight frown. "It's just that, after the Feast I must return to my father's lands. And then your grace leaves for Netar, and I don't know when I'll get the chance to—"

Aefric's attention was caught as a shadow moved to his left. He sensed no magic, but he was sure he'd seen movement among the bushes.

"Wait," he said, turning, moving one hand in front of Sighild to keep her from standing.

Something flickered through the air past Aefric. Struck Sighild, who moaned softly and collapsed. Feathers, stuck to her chest just below the collarbone.

A blow dart?

"Assassin!" Aefric yelled, and raised one hand to call the Brightstaff to him. With the other he conjured a barrier. A sparkling transparent field that would block further such attacks.

The real attack came from behind.

It had been years since a blade had last entered Aefric's body, but he'd never forgotten the sensation. Sharp, painful and surprisingly cold.

And yet, following that moment of cold, this time he felt as though fire spread outward from the wound.

Aefric could almost hear that fire, roaring over the chaos he'd caused among the dancers with his cry.

Leppina and Temat rushed in, weapons drawn. But they were spinning.

No. The world was spinning.

No. It wasn't. It was fading to black.

Aefric collapsed.

5

So hot. But so cold.
 Now hot again.
 The world, a place of darkness.
 Darkness.
 Cold darkness.
 No. Hot darkness again.
 Now stabbing, painful brightness. Worse than darkness. Nothing to see, but that stabbing...
 Stabbing...
 Shivering hot. Sweltering cold.
 Twitching, twitching, twitching—
 Cramp. A word designed to describe a discomfort. A locked muscle. Didn't begin to cover what those twitches became. They were, to cramps, what a great tsunami was to a ripple in bathwater.
 Heat returns. Blazing. His very bones sweating, sweating, sweating—
 Sweating icicles now. Solid block of blazing cold. Searing cold. Cold beyond...
 Cold beyond...
 Where did the cold go?

Horrible cold it was. Fiendish. Surely proof that Aefric had sunk into one of the thirteen hells.

The sixth? He thought it was the sixth that knew such cold.

But he could think? He could number the hells?

Did that mean a break in the cold? And the heat?

But there were no breaks. The cold and the heat were all. Eternal, their war.

If ... if both were gone, what did that mean?

Was this just the break afforded by some fell tormentor? Before visiting even worse tortures on Aefric?

Wait.

That sound. That rapid, fluttering sound...

So faint. And yet...

Something ... familiar about it...

Was that his heartbeat?

Was he...

Dare he hope it?

Was he ... alive?

Aefric's eyes dragged themselves open. Just a crack. No wider than slits. Still, the brightness of the room jabbed through his eyes. A sharp sting that ran to the back of his skull. Made him wince and groan.

Well, all right. The groan came from more than just that sting.

Aches.

Oh, so very many aches.

Now that he had some awareness of his body, Aefric realized that most of what he felt was stiffness. Painful stiffness. As though his body were encased in armor that had rusted into place, trapping him in an awkward pose.

And there was a deeper ache spreading out from a place on his back. The left side. Just under the ribs.

Everything about him hurt. Even his scalp.

In fact, the only thing that came close to feeling good was letting out that first, loud, rasping groan. It gave some kind of relief to his chest and throat and jaw.

"He's awake! Your grace!"

Deirdre's voice, but his eyes still couldn't make sense of the painful brightness that beat fresh pain through his skull with every rapid heartbeat.

She sounded close, though. And someone with lots of rough calluses grabbed his left hand. Likely her.

"Can you hear me?" Deirdre's voice again, sounding worried.

Wincing, and closing his eyes again, Aefric tried to nod. And from the way his neck muscles complained, he must've succeeded.

Footsteps. Lots of them. Approaching?

"Move back, please. *Everyone*. Move back."

Aefric knew that voice too. Bebara. His ducal physician, and a cleric of Nilasah, the goddess of compassion and the patron of healers.

Deirdre released Aefric's hand. He heard hushed whispers. And something else too. Something drumming and repetitive that wasn't his heart. It came from outside his body.

Rain?

But that didn't make sense. The skies had been so clear…

Wait. Bebara was here? She'd come to Asarchai from Water's End? Just how long had Aefric been unconscious?

He felt the healer's cool, strong hands. No calluses. Smooth. One hand on his clammy forehead, pushing him back down. Down onto a soft pillow.

Her other hand ran slowly down his chest.

His bare chest. He was naked. And he could feel sheets under him, but not on top of him.

Bebara was whispering something in a language Aefric didn't know.

"Excellent," she said. "We may need only one more effort." Her tone sharpened a bit. "Your grace? Can you turn over?"

Aefric coughed and cleared his throat, but still couldn't get any words out. He settled for nodding again, though it was an effort.

But rolling over? No. That was too much. He couldn't even lift a leg or shoulder very far.

"Beornric," Bebara said.

"I'll help," Deirdre said.

Two pairs of strong, rough hands now, gently turning Aefric onto his belly.

Wait. Aefric was naked on a bed. Deirdre was not only present, but physically moving him. Her hands on his naked body. And yet, she hadn't made so much as a single joke or uttered a word of innuendo?

Dear gods, he must be dying.

Well, that would explain the sense of sheer tension in the room. He felt as though there were a dozen other people in there with him, and every one of them holding their breath.

Well, not *every* one of them. *Bebara* was breathing. But she seemed to be the only one.

The rough hands retreated, and the smooth, cool hands returned. Bebara gently pressed several different spots along his spine, as though testing something before touching the wound.

None of those touches particularly bothered him. Was that good or bad?

Her hands moved to the wound then.

Frozen, those hands. Moving fragments of arctic ice. No, not just arctic. That sixth hell. Nerrazz.

He jerked away by reflex.

"Stay still, your grace," Bebara said, then began murmuring in another language again, tracing her freezing fingers over that wound.

"Yes," she said at last. "One more treatment ought to do it. Delwit, hand me the pearl." She clucked her tongue. "No, boy, the large one with the golden sheen. This is no mere concussion we're treating."

Something hard and round on his back then. The pearl? If so, it had to be as wide as Aefric's thumb was long. And it was warm, too. Especially after those hands.

Why, compared to those icy, healer's hands, the pearl felt a nice hot bath after a dip in freezing waters.

Bebara began to roll the pearl back and forth. A short enough distance that there was no way the pearl ever completed a full rotation. And all the while, she kept up this low, soft chant.

Aefric recognized only one word in that chant. Nilasah.

Strange, though, the sensations he began to feel.

It was as though something reached through the pearl into his body. Not painfully, though. Just a presence, moving through him. Spanning outwards to the limits of his skin, then sweeping back, though the wound, into the pearl.

The presence had a soothing quality. All that stiffness and tension seemed to be eroding with each wave of presence moving through him.

Sometime in there Aefric lost consciousness again.

Aefric only realized he'd lost consciousness because he became aware of waking up again.

This time was better.

He was tucked into a bed. Warm. Comfortable. With blankets. He could hear someone breathing gently nearby. Little to hear beyond that, though. Maybe someone moving around, in the next room?

If there had been rain earlier, it must've stopped.

Slowly, tentatively, he opened his eyes.

Bright sunlight came in through a wide, glass-paned window. Arched. And the walls and ceiling were plastered and painted white, with the Deepwater sigil done large on the wall facing him, near an open doorway.

Was this Water's End? The room was small and white and simple, but with a very nice red calinwood nightstand on one side — the Brightstaff standing beside it — and on the other, Deirdre sat in a solid calinwood chair.

Aefric tried to speak, but his throat and mouth were too dry. All that came out was a choking kind of cough.

"Your grace!" Deirdre said, turning quickly and taking his hand again, before turning to the open door and calling. "He's awake!"

Once more, Aefric heard boots rushing his way. Not as many, this time. And before they got there, Deirdre gave him a relieved smile.

"Your grace gave us quite a scare."

He realized then that she looked exhausted. Wan. Her eyes puffy. And her long braid had frayed in so many places that loose hairs danced around her face.

Aefric tried to say something about that, but those rushing people entered the room. Bebara in the lead. Ageless and vibrant Bebara, with her long, steely gray hair and her cleric's robes of Nilasah yellow.

At her heel, a shaven-headed youth in pale robes, who was doubtlessly an apprentice. Though that may not have been the word that clerics used.

Behind them, Aefric thought he saw Beornric, Yrsa, and Karbin, but Bebara arrived first and demanded his attention. She shooed Deirdre back, and gestured for the apprentice to give Aefric a small cup of water.

"Sip, your grace," she said. "Sip slowly until your mouth stops absorbing all the liquid. Then try swallowing a little." Louder, to everyone else, she added, "Stay back, please."

The water was cool, and sweet, and slightly minty.

Aefric finished the whole cup without needing to swallow. His mouth had just been that dry. But Bebara didn't seem surprised by that. She simply nodded once, and gestured to her apprentice for more.

With the second cup, Aefric was finally able to swallow. The water soothed the whole way down his throat.

"Please, your grace," Bebara said, "recite your titles for me."

Aefric cleared his throat. Sipped a little more water.

"I am Ser Aefric Brightstaff, Duke of Deepwater, and Baron of Netar. I want to say Knight of Armyr, too, to be complete, but I don't think that counts as a title."

His voice sounded stronger than he expected.

Bebara nodded once.

"What do you remember about your injury?"

The memories seemed to surface as he recited them.

"It was the second night of the Feast of Dereth Sehk. I was at the dance, on the roof of Herewyn's keep in Asarchai. Sighild and I had stepped into a nook for a little private conversation. We'd just sat on the benches when I saw a shadow move among the bushes."

He shook his head. "I tried to move Sighild back and investigate. But something flickered through the air." He shook himself. "That blow dart. Is she—"

"A sleeping poison," Beornric said in calming tones. "Nothing more. She was fine by morning."

"Good," Aefric said, relaxing. "I yelled a warning. Called the Brightstaff to me..."

Aefric frowned, looking at it now, standing beside the bed. "How did it get here?"

"It followed you, of course," Karbin said, sounding like Aefric's mentor again, amused when the student missed an obvious answer.

"Please," Bebara said. "No more questions, your grace, until the recitation is complete. Your grace called his weapon to him. What next?"

"With my other hand" — Aefric raised his left hand, surprised at how easy it was to do so — "I raised a shield against missile weapons. But with my whole attention that direction, I was stabbed from behind."

"Tell me about the stabbing. Not the location or any of that drivel. Tell me what it felt like. Compared to other stabbings your grace has received, for I know this was not the first."

"Not the fifth, either," Aefric said, pleased that he'd managed to sound droll. "Usually, the sensation of a blade entering my body is cold. And it was this time too. At first. But then fire seemed to blaze outward from the blade. Into me."

"You felt this fire," Bebara said. "Did you sense it any other way? Did you see flames, for example?"

"No," Aefric said, frowning. "But I heard them."

"Good," Bebara said, with a nod. "I read the poison correctly then.

Your grace was stabbed with a blade that must have been *dripping* with dweomerbane."

"Dweomerbane?" Deirdre said, sounding outraged.

"That's right," Bebara said to Deirdre. "You are a dweomerblade. So I will allow you this one interruption."

She turned back to Aefric.

"Is your grace familiar with the poison?"

Aefric shook his head.

"It was developed during the Godswalk Wars. It targets the magic inherent in a dweomerblade and uses it to burn them to death from the inside."

"How did I survive?"

"Honestly?" she asked. "You shouldn't have. You obviously received at least one full dose of the poison, possibly more. And as powerful as your grace is, he should have died within ... no more than fifty breaths. Possibly twenty."

But Beornric was smiling. "Does your grace remember dancing with a woman named Jodella?"

Aefric frowned, but Bebara nodded as though her question had been answered.

"Yes," Aefric said slowly. "Large woman, with a lot of wild, curly hair, I think?"

"That's her," Beornric said. "It seems she was the last woman your grace danced with before seeking someplace quiet with Sighild. So she was nearby when the attack came."

Beornric stepped closer, smiling wider now.

"Good thing, too," he said. "She happens to be Motte's county physician. She answered the call for aid almost as fast as this one did."

He nodded to Deirdre, but Deirdre didn't preen as she usually would.

"I was too slow," she said. "I should've been closer. I should've been ready. I—"

"Enough," Beornric barked. "His grace owes you his life, Deirdre. Without your quick actions, even Bebara here could

not have saved him. I'll not have you acting as though you failed."

Deirdre frowned as Beornric turned to Aefric and continued.

"Your grace, there were two assassins. Professionals. A team. The first was the distraction. He was the one who put Sighild to sleep. He was also the one found and killed quickly by Leppina and Temat."

He nodded towards Deirdre.

"She was the only one who realized there was a second assassin. Blade poised to finish the job. And he would have, too, if not for her. But Deirdre dispatched him with admirable speed. And more than a little fury."

"He dared attack my ... duke," Deirdre said quietly, still not sounding like herself.

"How did you spot him, Deirdre?" Aefric asked. "And why didn't Leppina and Temat?"

"He was disguised with magic," she said. "But it wasn't invisibility or any kind of illusion. It was a blending spell."

Understanding washed over Aefric. "Which is from the clay and stone branch of magic."

"Exactly," she said. "Which, I suspect, was why your grace didn't feel the assassin settling into place. His small magic was hidden by the sense of Burrow's stronger magic. But when he struck—"

"When he struck," Aefric said, "his magic had to work harder to hide him. Became easier to notice."

"Especially since I was looking for it," she said, then frowned. "I wish I could kill him twice."

"You may yet be able to," Yrsa said. "Metaphorically speaking. Whoever sent that assassin is still out there."

"Am I done then?" Bebara asked. "Am I being dismissed?"

"No," Aefric said, managing a half-smile. "I think your work comes first right now."

Bebara whisked everyone else back out of the room — including Deirdre — and gave Aefric a thorough examination. Which mostly involved touching him here and there, while praying. Sometimes her touch felt cold, other times hot, and each time, he was to tell her.

When she finished, she said, "All right. Your grace will live. Though I will wish him to drink a potion I'll brew for him each morning for the next aett."

"I'll be sure to drink it."

"And though your grace will feel stronger in a day or so, your grace is not to exert himself. At least until he's drunk the eighth and final draught of that potion."

"I'll be good," Aefric said, smiling.

"I include spellcasting in this," she said, raising a warning finger. "For the next aett you are to attempt nothing more demanding than you would *honestly* expect an apprentice to accomplish."

That would be harder, but so was the look in Bebara's eye.

Aefric nodded. "I'll … control the impulse to do more."

"Thank you, your grace," she said, then opened a drawer in the nightstand. "Now before I leave, your grace should see something."

What she pulled out of the drawer was round, dark brown, and so very dry it was spider-webbed with cracks. It looked like a small, desiccated wooden ball.

"This, your grace, was once a gold-sheened pearl."

A pearl? That thing was almost big enough to fill Aefric's *palm*.

She set in on the nightstand.

She reached into the drawer and pulled out another. Held it up significantly, and set it beside the first.

She did this three more times, until five such husks sat on the nightstand.

"Your grace lives," she said, "because Jodella was swift enough and skilled enough and *smart* enough to know she could not save him. She placed your grace in suspension, where he remained until Karbin was recalled from Kivash to magically transport your grace here to me. Where I had the resources to do what she could not."

She gestured to the ex-pearls. "Golden-sheened pearls. Of sufficient size and quantity to allow me to filter *all* of the poison from not only your grace's body, but his *power*. The only way to defeat dweomerbane, stop the damage from spreading, and allow healing to begin."

She folded her arms.

"This treatment is quite difficult. And as your grace can probably imagine, quite expensive." She managed to look even sterner. "Now, I realize that your grace is one of the wealthiest men in this part of the continent. And yet, I ask that your grace keep in mind that pearls as rare as these are not quickly replaced, even for the rich."

"In other words, don't let this happen again?"

"Very good, your grace," she said, with a fierce smile. "I shall take my leave now and send in your grace's very worried advisers."

AEFRIC MANAGED TO PROP HIMSELF UP ON THE BED ENOUGH TO FEEL AS though he were sitting. Though, in truth, he was slumping.

Still. He supposed that was close enough. He was still in a bed he hadn't known he had, in a private room he hadn't realized existed.

He supposed he should've known that the duke would have a special healing room in the physician's offices here at Water's End. The castle was large enough that he probably had rooms for anything he could think of, and he still hadn't seen close to half of the place.

But the glass windows brought in encouraging sunshine, if not a breeze. And the smell in here wasn't antiseptic, like part of him kept expecting from his experiences with hospitals in another world.

No, in here the smell was flowery and pleasant. Slightly of peonies.

Aefric should have been hungry. He knew that. He could even feel a rumble in his stomach. And yet, staring at those five, huge, dried out husks that had once been golden pearls, he found he had no appetite.

He was still staring at those husks when the others came in.

Beornric and Yrsa, both wearing dark tunics and hose — his more of a brown, and hers more of a very dark red.

In Yrsa's case, the color brought out the reds in her hair and in that major scar of hers. The one that drew a line down the left side of her face, right through the eye, which was left a shade of red itself, by the healers' efforts to save it.

Karbin, in his colors of sand and dusk, with three wands on his belt, and that strange, obsidian rod of his. Karbin's skin wasn't much lighter in shade than that rod, and still glowed with the bloom of youth, even though the man had to be at least two or three times Aefric's age.

A side benefit to mastery of wizardry, his youthful appearance.

Deirdre followed them in. She had fixed her hair, and doing so seemed to give her a little of her swagger back. Although she looked now as though she had a lot of anger and just wanted a place to vent it.

"Deirdre," Beornric said, "there are matters the three of us must go over with his grace. Perhaps—"

"One moment," Aefric said. "Deirdre, if you would come closer?"

She stepped up and bowed. "I am at your command, your grace."

She bowed. She didn't kneel. And there was nothing flirty or teasing in her tone or her word choice.

"Deirdre," he said, "you *do* realize that you didn't fail me, do you not?"

"Those assassins should never have gotten close to your grace," she said. "I should have demanded to search the roof myself before his arrival. I should have—"

"Enough," Aefric said.

She grimaced, but bowed.

"Deirdre," he said, in what he hoped were soothing tones, "any demands about security would have had to come from Beornric, not you. And if he'd made such demands as you just began to list, he would have been insulting the baroness and her people."

Deirdre arched a dark red eyebrow. "Then perhaps her lordship should've been insulted."

Aefric chuckled, and for just a moment he saw a spark of Deirdre's normal self in her eyes.

"No," Aefric said. "In fact, I expect that Herewyn is excoriating her commanders and soldiers for allowing me to come that close to getting killed while in her care."

Aefric raised a hand for silence before she could reply.

"Herewyn knows I'm alive?" Aefric asked Beornric.

"Kentigern sent out rikas once Bebara declared your grace out of danger," Beornric said. "All of your important vassals have been informed, as has his majesty."

"If we're going to talk about that," Yrsa started, but Aefric shook his head.

"Not yet," he said, and turned back to Deirdre. "Please forgive my distraction. As I was saying, I am very proud of my knights. Leppina and Temat reacted swiftly and did their job. And I intend to thank them personally, later. And as for you..."

She glanced at Aefric, something like muted hope in her jade green eyes.

He smiled and shook his head in wonder.

"Once more, Deirdre," he said, "you managed to go above and beyond. As you always seem to. Once again, you sensed what others missed, and accomplished more than I could dare ask."

Deirdre frowned, looking caught between smiling at the compliment, and her self-recriminations.

"You were instrumental in saving my life," Aefric said. "And you bear no blame in the fact that my life needed saving."

She frowned as though she might object.

"*Ser Deirdre Ol'Miri,*" Aefric snapped. "I am your liege, and I am *telling* you that you bear no blame in the matter of the attempt on my life."

"Yes, your grace," she said, bowing again.

"And there's something more," Aefric said.

"Your grace?" she asked, looking honestly curious.

"I've been meaning to do this for quite some time now. You've more than earned it." He shook his head, giving her a chagrined smile. "I don't have the badge here, so we can do this formally later."

"Your grace?" she asked, with hope in those jade green eyes.

"Ser Deirdre Ol'Miri," Aefric said, "I would name you my ducal champion."

"Thank you, your grace!" she said, and now she did take one knee, giving Aefric the purest smile he'd seen from her since he'd woken up.

"And as I expect my champion to keep herself in excellent shape, I suggest you see about both food and sleep."

"Yes, your grace," Deirdre said, with an embarrassed smile. "At once."

She stood and turned to leave, but before she could, Aefric said, "And Deirdre?"

"Yes, your grace?" she said, turning back.

"Thank you for your vigil," he said. "As I woke, it was a great comfort to realize you were nearby. Because it meant I was safe."

Her posture straightened, shoulders back again, chest out proudly once more. She looked herself again. But the smile she gave Aefric still wasn't her usual tease. It was … more personal, but no less sincere.

"Always, your grace," she said. "I will stand between your grace and harm to my last breath. And beyond, if I am able."

Then she bowed, turned and left.

AEFRIC SMILED AS DEIRDRE LEFT HIS RECOVERY ROOM. THOUGH THAT did mean that he was now alone with Yrsa, Beornric and Karbin. So as much as he wanted to rest right then — and exhaustion was taking its toll — he knew he had at least one matter to deal with first.

The assassins.

"That was well done, your grace," Yrsa said, and Aefric caught something about her tone. Like a shift in the wind that portended a storm. "*She* bore no blame for the attempt on your life. And she certainly shouldn't blame herself that way."

"I'm glad you agree," Aefric said, tentatively.

"Sadly," she continued, "I cannot say the same for your grace."

"What do you—"

She tossed a bracer onto Aefric's bed.

Oh. Apparently they *weren't* going to talk about the assassins yet.

It looked like a simple bronze bracer, to be worn about the bicep. But this bracer was magical. Something he had gotten from Duke Wylyn's wizard, Sifwyn...

"When I learned the details of that attack on your grace, it made no sense," Yrsa said. "At least, not until I asked Dajen to check your rooms. He discovered *this* among your grace's jewelry. Not on his person. Where it belonged."

"Why," Beornric asked, picking up from Yrsa, for the two worked well together, "was that bracer here at Water's End, and not *on your grace's person*?"

Aefric sighed. They were both right, of course. The magic of that bracer turned aside blades and arrows.

"You do realize," Aefric said, "that even the enchantments on that bracer aren't foolproof against assass—"

"They're right," Karbin said, cutting in smoothly. "Even if that bracer didn't force the assassin to miss, it might've turned a deep stab wound into a grazing cut. With significantly less poison going into your system."

"Why, your grace," Beornric said, his voice like restrained thunder, "was this bracer here at Water's End and not on your arm? Where it *should've* been?"

"Sifwyn's arms are smaller," Aefric said, "I never got around to—"

"*Aefric,*" Karbin said, angrily.

"Does your grace realize," Yrsa asked, in surprisingly casual tones, "just how difficult it is to restrain myself from beating some sense into his noble person?"

Likely just a threat. *Likely* Yrsa wouldn't *actually* give Aefric a beating. After all, he *was* her liege.

Still. Even the thought that she *might* do it was sobering. Gods knew the woman stood even taller than Aefric, and had a scary kind of strength. Especially in her hands.

"Enough," Aefric said. "Point made. Hand it here."

Yrsa picked up the bracer and tossed it to Aefric. He caught it and put it on his left arm.

After all, it was an *enchanted* bracer. It immediately adjusted to fit him. As it did, he felt its protective magic settle into place.

"Good," Beornric said. "I hope we can count on it *remaining* there. Especially when your grace is in public?"

"To be sure of that," Yrsa said, giving Aefric a look that said the beating wasn't off the table yet, "I think his grace should explain why he wasn't wearing it in the first place."

"I *would* be interested in the answer," Karbin said.

Aefric drew a deep breath.

"Ever since the king created me Duke of Deepwater, you two" — Aefric nodded to Beornric and Yrsa — "have been emphasizing that I need to act and think like a duke, not an adventurer."

"Don't blame this on us," Yrsa said.

"I'm not blaming anyone or making excuses," Aefric said, his own patience beginning to wane. "I'm *explaining reasoning*. So I expect you to let me finish."

Yrsa's chin jerked with a rough nod.

"When I was an adventurer, I would have put this bracer on the moment I knew what it did." Aefric saw Karbin nod absently, in agreement. "After all, I lived a life of never-ending threats and challenges. If I found a bracer like this one in a room in an ancient keep, I might need its magic in the very next room."

Aefric shook his head.

"But now I'm a duke. I'm supposed to have others take those risks *for* me."

Karbin's eyes widened, and he nodded once. He understood. Of course, he'd known Aefric the longest. And like Aefric, he was a former adventurer.

But Yrsa and Beornric didn't get it yet. So Aefric kept talking.

"That's not easy for me. It goes against a lifetime of habit. But I've been trying. And one of the hardest things for me to do is, in the moment, assess which risks I *should* take and which I *shouldn't*."

He patted the cold bronze bracer, now on his arm.

"This bracer makes me safer. More than that, I knew that wearing it would make me *feel* safer. Which would throw off my risk-assessment."

"Ah," Beornric said, and drew a long, slow breath. "This is very much like what we were talking about before, isn't it? About how you shouldn't risk yourself for your knights, even if they might die."

Aefric nodded. "I was going to avoid wearing this until I'd developed the habit of acting and thinking like a duke first and foremost. *Then* I figured it would be safe for me to wear the bracer, because it wouldn't make me more likely to do something … questionable."

Yrsa cocked her head and narrowed her eyes at Aefric.

"That hardly agrees with your own recounting of the attempt on your life, your grace. The moment you spotted the blow dart, you immediately cast a spell that would have turned more blow darts aside."

"Of course."

"So the only difference between that spell and that bracer is that you would need a moment to cast the spell."

"No," Aefric said. "First, the bracer also turns aside blades." He frowned. "It might turn away maces and other weapons. I'd have to check the magic. But second, you're overlooking a key difference."

Yrsa stared, stonily, as she waited.

"The spell is a decision. I have to cast it. Which means that before I cast it, I have a moment in which I could decide if I'm about to follow the right course of action, or the wrong one."

"Ah," Yrsa said, long and slow. "I see it now. The bracer would encourage your old instincts."

Aefric nodded.

"And now?" Yrsa asked. "Now that you *barely* survived an assassination attempt that might have been *prevented entirely* by that little chunk of spelled bronze? What is your grace's opinion about the bracer *now*?"

"I need to wear it," Aefric said, remembering what Duke Wylyn had told him only a few aetts ago. "After all, it's the attack I *don't* see that could kill me."

"Beornric, Karbin," Yrsa said, "I believe we've made our point. Shall we leave our dear duke to his rest?"

Karbin and Beornric readily agreed, and all three left, looking entirely too pleased with themselves.

But in the moment, Aefric couldn't care about that. He was too busy falling back asleep.

After one more check from Bebara, Aefric was allowed to dress and return to his own rooms. Though that was a long enough walk up so many flights of stairs in the immense castle that was Water's End that it might've counted as exertion.

Of course, flying *definitely* would have counted as exertion. So walking it was. With breaks at every landing.

Took longer than he liked to think about.

He dined in his own rooms that night, and he slept in his own bed. In fact, the only thing of any significance that he did over the remainder of that day was personally thank Leppina and Temat for their roles in saving his life.

Of course, like Deirdre, they'd been inclined to blame themselves for the attempt, rather than accept thanks for foiling it. But Aefric was pretty sure he got the point across.

The next morning, Aefric dressed in simple clothes, for a duke. A navy blue tunic over Deepwater gray hose. Belt and shoes of dark leather, with the usual accompaniments.

He did intend to return to work in a limited capacity, though. Starting with his customary daily meeting with his advisers. Although rather than its usual location — the meeting room in his apartments — he held it out on the large balcony on the public floor of his apartments.

After all, it was a beautiful day. Warm, but not too warm, with a gentle breeze that suggested rain would come by nightfall. A suggestion emphasized by the storm clouds coming up from the south.

Those clouds weren't here yet, though. Up above, the skies were pale blue and beautiful. An interesting contrast to the perfect navy blue of the castle walls, shimmering as they did as though they were sculpted from the depths of Lake Deepwater down below.

Plenty of traffic out on the lake that day. Ships coming and going from the port down below, while smaller fishing boats and pleasure craft set about their own business.

They all looked so small from here. Aefric's apartments were high up in the keep itself. Nothing on the Seven Great Spires around him, of course, but still, a couple of hundred feet above the docks.

His balcony on this level was large enough that he could have thrown a decent party without it feeling crowded. And the furniture was elegantly carved greenwood, with the chairs comfortably padded.

He was sitting on one of those chairs, at a large, round table, when his advisers began to arrive.

Yrsa and Beornric first. Yrsa in dark riding leathers and a dark leather doublet over a light tan tunic. As usual, she wore both those huge maces of hers, one riding on each hip.

Beornric wore a dark red quilted tunic over dark orange hose, with his longsword hanging from his leather belt.

Both wore their customary heavy boots.

Kentigern Ol'Klimath, Aefric's seneschal, followed, accompanied by Ser Garnotin Artaretek, Aefric's new castellan.

A position Aefric had needed to fill after he learned that his last castellan — Ser Calder, who'd served going back to when the Soulfists ruled Deepwater — had been stealing from the nobility and passing shipping information on to the pirate queen, Nelazzi.

Calder had managed to flee capture. For now.

Kentigern wore a quilted tunic of royal blue, trimmed in silver, with hose the color of dark mustard, and those low, soft leather boots he favored, because they had silver thread among the black, turned-down cuffs.

He was one of those rare Armyrian nobles with tanned skin, which might've been part of the reason he wore his dark beard so think and full. To lend him a little pallor.

He wasn't wearing his black velvet cap today, which Aefric took as a good sign. Kentigern always seemed to have bad news when he was wearing that hat.

Ser Garnotin was a dark-skinned man of middle years. He'd be tall in most rooms, but he wasn't quite as tall as Aefric, and certainly not as tall as Yrsa.

Like Beornric, Garnotin held his age well, and still looked strong enough to hold a bridge against a small army. As rumor claimed he'd done once, in his youth. Certainly the warhammer he wore on his back looked menacing enough.

His tunic today was a bright purple, over dark orange hose.

Elkari Ol'Nuval, Aefric's historian, arrived next, carrying stacks of scrolls in her ink-stained hands, as she did so often. Though one of those hands was pushing her dark hair out of her eyes.

Odd, that. She usually wore her hair quite short.

Elkari wore breeches and tunic today, in dark browns that went well with her dusky complexion.

Last to arrive was Karbin, in his robes the colors of sand and dusk. Today he carried his obsidian rod in one hand, and he wore no wands on his belt at all.

Once everyone was seated — without any of the formality games, for Aefric eschewed formality at his morning meetings — Aefric said, "Let's start with the assassins. What do we know?"

"Very little so far," Yrsa said, frowning.

"A rika arrived from Armityr this morning," Kentigern said. "His majesty has declared the attempt on your grace as related to the recent attempts on the royal family."

"So the royal investigator will be handling it then?"

"Yes," Kentigern said, visibly struggling not to add Aefric's courtesy. "Although your grace is, of course, permitted to assign someone to assist and coordinate with the royal investigation."

"I think they're wrong," Beornric said. "The method was different. The other assassins had all been placed in positions to get close to their targets. The assassins in Asarchai weren't part of any detachment."

"Do we have any reason to think they were or were not affiliated with the Order of the Severed Dream?" Aefric asked.

"They weren't," Beornric said. "Neither assassin was carrying the signature flame-shaped dagger."

"Then what makes his majesty think the attacks are related?" Aefric asked. "All the other assassins used that dagger. Or at least had it on them."

"Unknown," Beornric said. "Perhaps his majesty has information we do not?"

Garnotin scoffed. "Or perhaps his majesty is playing politics with his grace's life."

"His majesty values our duke's life almost as highly as his own," Beornric said.

"The link is obvious," Yrsa said, drawing the attention of the others. "Outside of the royal family, his grace is the most prominent noble in Armyr."

That brought a quick round of disagreements and debates from Aefric's advisers about the influence of Duke Wylyn and the sheer power and history of Duchess Ashling, but Yrsa came in over the top of them, vocally.

"Let me speak." When she had silence, she continued. "His grace has held his title for a little more than a season, and he has already won a war for Armyr. Without any losses on our side. Then he proceeded to save the lives of the king and queen. Shall I go on?"

No one spoke.

"Matters of wealth, influence and power may be debated," Yrsa said. "But right now, our duke's *name* is spoken farther and wider than that of any other Armyrian noble."

"Which makes him a target," Garnotin said, nodding. "I agree."

"Besides," Yrsa said. "The same person can hire masons from different guilds for different jobs. That's no less true for assassins."

"Nevertheless," Aefric said, "we might be wise to consider the possibility that someone else was behind the attempt on my life."

"What do you have in mind?" Yrsa asked.

"I think we should assign a knight to aid the royal investigation.

Garnotin take your pick for this from the younger knights who show potential."

"I have someone in mind already," Garnotin said with a nod.

"Meanwhile," Yrsa said, one eyebrow raised, "you intend to assign someone else to investigate the attempt?"

"I see no reason not to. The person I have in mind shouldn't interfere with the royal investigation."

"She certainly does feel motivated," Yrsa said, clearly knowing who Aefric had in mind.

"I advise against this," Kentigern said. "The investigation has been declared the province of the royal investigator."

"An order that arrived today?" Aefric asked.

"Yes, your grace."

"Pity, then," Aefric said with a smile, "that I assigned her this task as soon as I awoke yesterday. Now, of course, she's unreachable by rika, and I'm not sure where she is."

Beornric, Yrsa, Karbin and Garnotin all nodded agreement. Elkari simply frowned, considering. But Kentigern looked as though he'd eaten bad mussels.

"Risky," he said.

"She has my complete confidence," Aefric said, then sighed. "And I think his majesty may be looking in the wrong direction this time."

"Why?" Kentigern said, then quickly added, "If I may ask?"

"Nelazzi," Yrsa said, and Aefric nodded, so she continued. "She's been trying to expand her piracy into slavery, and our duke here has been interfering. And now she doesn't even have her informant at Water's End anymore, because Calder had to flee."

"And the last thing she would have known for certain from Calder's reports," Beornric said, "was that your grace intended to attend the Feast of Dereth Sehk."

"That's my thinking," Aefric said. "Any disagreements?"

"Only one," Karbin said, and all eyes turned to him. "Either give me this assignment, or allow me to work with her."

"Close, old friend," Aefric said with a smile. "I want you to approach this from the other direction. Investigate Nelazzi's activities and her people. Coordinate with Deirdre by spell, and together you should be able to bring back answers without tripping over each other's boots."

"I *have* worked with people before," Karbin said, drolly. "Perhaps you remember?"

"I do, of course," Aefric said. "But both you and Deirdre are both used to handling this kind of investigation alone. This is an instance where more might not be better."

Karbin opened his mouth the answer that, but Aefric raised one hand.

"*But*," he said quickly, "let me offer this compromise. You and she will talk before you both leave. Work out for yourselves how you can best make this work. I want results, and I want you both back alive. Even if it means wounding your pride in the process."

Karbin acquiesced with a nod.

"Now," Aefric said, rubbing his hands together. "What's next?"

THAT MORNING MEETING LASTED ALL THE WAY THROUGH LUNCH. THERE was just too much to cover. From the usual preparations for the coming harvest — and attendant Harvest Festival — to the rebuilding efforts.

Especially along the coast, where the storms would be worse, and the threat of Nelazzi's ships worse still.

But his advisers were gone about their tasks now, the day was beautiful, and Aefric found his greenwood chair on his public floor balcony quite comfortable, for a man who needed rest more than he wanted to admit. Combined with the lingering taste of delicious roast duck from lunch, all in all, he felt full and relaxed.

So when Deirdre arrived in response to his summons, he welcomed her there on the balcony.

Deirdre seemed much more herself today. Her braid sharp, her new badge of office — the Deepwater sigil, done in gold — pinned to her dark maroon armor, near the left shoulder. She had a little color in her cheeks, and a playful smile in those jade eyes as she knelt before Aefric.

"You want me, your grace?" she asked.

They were alone, so Aefric chuckled at her phrasing, which made her smile.

"Have a seat, Deirdre," he said, gesturing to a chair.

She lingered on her knees for a moment, smiling as though she considered saying something, but took the offered seat.

"Are you hungry?" he asked. "Thirsty? I can have something brought."

"Nothing for me, your grace."

"His majesty has decided that the attempt on my life is part of the series of attempts that were made on the royal family."

"His majesty ... knows best, of course," Deirdre said.

"I think his majesty may be mistaken in this case."

"So do I, your grace," she said firmly.

Aefric chuckled again.

"So," he said. "His majesty has assigned the matter to his royal investigator. I have Garnotin assigning some competent young knight to coordinate from our end."

"Oh?" Deirdre said, and a smile played about the corners of her mouth. Perhaps she saw where this was going.

"Yes," Aefric said. "Unfortunately, his majesty's orders didn't arrive until today. But when I first awoke yesterday, I immediately assigned my best investigator to find out who was behind the attempt on my life. You left at once, of course."

"Of course, your grace," Deirdre said, preening a bit at the praise. "And naturally I have to stay out of touch during the investigation."

"Naturally," Aefric said.

"I have a friend who can get my name on the passenger list of a ship that left for Ajenmoor yesterday," she said. "Just in case anyone checks."

"Not Ajenmoor," Aefric said. "I could reach Ajenmoor by rika to within an hour or two, and it wouldn't be believable that you'd left there already."

"Good point, your grace." She chewed her lip a moment, and Aefric was surprised how fetching he found the little gesture. "Make it Behal. So many boats and ships travel between here and there that no one could prove I didn't. Plus, by the time his majesty's orders came through, I'd have been well gone by horse, leaving no word about where I was going."

"That will work," Aefric said. "One other thing."

"Yes, your grace?" she asked with an eager look.

"Before you actually leave, speak with Karbin. I suspect Nelazzi's hand may be behind this—"

"My thoughts exactly, your grace."

"—and he can approach the question from the other end. Finding out what Nelazzi and her people have been doing of late. With him working that end, and you working from the assassins themselves..."

"We should have an answer even faster," Deirdre said, nodding. "And he knows the contact spell, so we can coordinate safely at predetermined times."

"So you don't mind working with a partner in this?"

"Not where your grace's safety is involved," she said, her tone serious. "Speaking of which, should we suspect Kefthal?"

"Not at this point," Aefric said. "I think they're playing a deeper game. Just sending assassins after me feels too ... simple for them." He shook his head. "But don't rule them out. I don't want to limit your thinking."

"Understood," she said. "Is there anything more?"

"One thing," Aefric said, and quirked a half-smile. "Do whatever you have to, to come back alive. I don't want to lose you over this."

"Yes, your grace," Deirdre said with a small smile.

"I guess that's it then," Aefric said. "You should probably get going."

"Of course, your grace," she said, standing, but then hesitated. Frowned just a little.

"Is something on your mind, Deirdre?"

"Yes, your grace," she said, chewing her lip again for a moment before adding, "may I speak freely?"

"Don't you always?" Aefric asked with a chuckle, but then said, "Please. By all means."

"I know full well that I could never be a fit bride for your grace," she said. "I have no wealth. No title. No family name worth mentioning. I could boast a great deed or two, but I couldn't pretend that would be enough. Not to mention how *terrible* I'd be at all the politicking and socializing."

She laughed, but not with humor.

"But I will promise your grace this. I will keep both eyes on whatever bride he chooses. So that if she ever betrays him" — her jade eyes glistened — "if she ever betrays you, Aefric, I swear by all the gods that she will answer for that betrayal. Even if I must hunt for her through every one of the thirteen hells, and carve my way to her through a horde of demons."

"Thank you, Deirdre," Aefric said softly, touched by the depth of feeling in her words. "For what it's—"

"Please, your grace," she said quickly, "don't. I don't need a response to that. I ... I just needed your grace to know."

Aefric nodded.

She quirked a half-smile then that managed to dislodge a tear and send it trickling down her cheek.

"Of course," she said, "your grace also should know that if he ever desires the noble privilege, I shall most happily ruin him for all other women."

"That's quite a bold claim," Aefric said through a chuckle.

Deirdre cocked an eyebrow and a hip. "I make many bold claims, your grace. Which of them have I failed to fulfill?"

"None," Aefric conceded. "You've proven all of them true so far."

She nodded firmly. "And your grace may rest assured that, given the chance, I shall give *this* bold claim the same degree of focus and effort."

"Fair enough," Aefric said, smiling. "Come back alive from this mission and I'll call you to my chambers that very night."

"Now *there's* motivation," she said softly. But then tried for a teasing tone, though it sounded a little forced. "I understand that Duchess Ashling of Merrek may be making bastards fashionable—"

"Deirdre."

"I'm just saying, your grace," she said, sounding more like herself again. "Looks. Power. Finesse. Our child would have it all."

And somehow she had him laughing again. Honestly, openly laughing. How did she do that?

"Fine," Aefric said. "If I ever find I need a bastard, I'll keep you in mind."

"Then my work here is done," she said, smiling as she bowed. "I'll return as soon as possible with my findings."

"I know you will," Aefric said.

She left then.

Aefric stood and, leaning on the Brightstaff more than he liked, walked to the rail to look over the lake.

So many ships and boats out on the lake. Like little reminders of all the things he had to do. Visit his barony in Netar. Stop by the capital on his way there or his way back. Prepare his lands and people for winter. And more. So much more.

All this, knowing that the kingdom might soon be at war with Caiperas. At least, pending findings of the royal investigator.

Where did Nelazzi fit into all this? And Kefthal? And Malimfar, for that matter?

So many questions. But Aefric couldn't get answers right now. No. Right now he had to rest, and heal.

With that in mind, he turned, and went back inside. He needed to take a nap before dinner.

Doubtless, in light of Aefric's near death, Beornric would want to revisit the topic of bridal candidates.

And despite her own words, Aefric found himself thinking that perhaps that list should include the name Deirdre Ol'Miri.

SIGN UP FOR STEFON'S NEWSLETTER

Stefon loves to keep in touch with his readers, and loves to keep you reading. The best way for him to do both is for you to sign up for his newsletter.

Sign up at http://www.stefonmears.com/join

If you sign up for Stefon's newsletter, you get...

- Monthly updates about his publishing and travel schedules
- His latest news, in brief, and answers to reader questions
- A free short story for signing up
- List-only offers and occasional specials
- Plus a free short story every month!

ABOUT THE AUTHOR

Stefon Mears has attended some strange rites in his day. Stefon has more than thirty books to his credit, and he never stops writing. He earned his M.F.A. in Creative Writing from N.I.L.A., and his B.A. in Religious Studies (double emphasis in Ritual and Mythology) from U.C. Berkeley. He's a lifelong gamer and fantasy fan. Stefon lives in Portland, Oregon, with his wife and three cats.

Look for Stefon online:
www.stefonmears.com
himself@stefonmears.com

Lightning Source UK Ltd.
Milton Keynes UK
UKHW010635221222
414292UK00013B/337/J